Your Undercover Brother

An Able Body Mystery

J. Salvatore Domino

For permissions contact: info@stairns.com

Published in the United States
by
Stairns Media Publishing, Scottsdale, Arizona
www.Stairns.com

Title: Your Undercover Brother / J. Salvatore Domino
Description: First Edition

ISBN 979-8-9880034-1-0 (Paperback)

MY ONLY HOPE

Slumped by the side of a winding rural road about a half-mile outside the Stoney Brook Wildlife Sanctuary just a few feet off the pavement, I knelt hunched over in pain, my knees grinding into the gravel, my eyes trying to adjust to the dim light cast by the waning crescent moon. I struggled in vain to make sense of what had just unfolded.

On my left, smoke rose from a ditch on the side of the roadway. Strong odors of burning oil and melting rubber emanated from the remains of a late-model luxury sports car. The limited-edition pearl white paint and chrome wheels were now a blackened heap of scrap.

Still trapped inside the passenger compartment was my former girlfriend, Jessica Sekelsky-McGleam

How I crawled away from that wreckage is anybody's guess. I called out weakly for help, but there was no one nearby, no one to help. Unable to do more, I prayed someone would find us before it was too late.

Then, as if sent from heaven, a car appeared. Its bright headlights approached the scene slowly. Unable to stand, I raised my hand, mewling out. "Call for help. Call an ambulance."

The driver stopped, paused briefly, peered through the open passenger window at the wreckage, then inexplicably sped away.

"No, wait," I cried. Watching as the car drove away. "Please stop."

Shocked that they would just leave us in distress, I collapsed on the ground. Without help, it seemed today would be our last day on earth.

It was probably only minutes, but it seemed like an eternity until a police patrol car and two fire trucks arrived on the scene. Somehow, the car's electronics must have alerted the authorities.

Seconds later, flashing red and blue lights blinded me as car after car of law enforcement vehicles screeched to a halt, blocking the roadway and illuminating the dark asphalt.

As they surrounded the smoking wreck, a company of rescue workers scurried about, shouting instructions while a team of firefighters and Emergency Medical Technicians used the jaws of life to pull Jessica's body from the wreckage.

A hundred feet away, in both directions, a half dozen county and state police officers waved flashlights and placed barriers around the scene. Police officers from the other nearby small towns fanned out to direct traffic, commanding gawking passersby and rubberneckers to go about their business.

The noise and confusion of the emergency response added to my already overpowering misery.

I watched in stunned, helpless silence amid the crushing pain that consumed me. Only twenty feet away, a pair of paramedics used exotic-looking black boxes to check Jessica's vital signs. One barked critical data into the radio, while the other examined her body for signs of trauma.

The paramedics ignored me. As if I did not matter. Perhaps they felt between the two of us, Jessica's injuries were more severe. That her life was in more danger. Or they looked at Jessica in her Givenchy slacks and Gucci top, then looked at me in my off-brand sneakers and worn blue jeans I bought on clearance from Mega-Mart. Maybe they decided she was more worth saving?

But they didn't know the entire story. Only Jessica and I knew what happened here tonight. Would it be different if they knew the truth?

As I lay there watching the paramedics work to save Jessica's life, two uniformed police officers pointed toward me, still lying on the ground writhing in agony. One shrugged, the other nodded. They both laughed as they debated what to do next. I thought, "How could they laugh about anything that was happening here?"

Seconds later, a burly, barrel-chested county police officer approached. "Sir, Norfolk County Sheriff's Police. You will have to come with us."

"Officer, I am hurt," I mumbled. "I need to go to the hospital."

Unmoved, the officer repeated. "Sir, you will have to come with me."

As they lifted Jessica onto a gurney and into the ambulance, my head started spinning. Then everything went black.

The next thing I knew, I was alone in the rear compartment of a beat-up police transport van. Two police officers occupied the cab, chatting each other up like they were on lunch break. Thick black nylon cable ties secured my hands and feet, which were strapped together behind my back. One small glass porthole between the front driver's cab and my chamber illuminated the otherwise blackness of the unlit steel cube. The combination of the cold metal and the evening chill quickly took hold, sending shivers through my body.

With nothing restraining me, each time the van changed speed, I slid from side to side and from back to front inside the steel box. As the driver sped along the winding road, every change in direction resulted in a painful thump. When he slammed on the brakes, I flew forward into the metal framework inside the cabin, bashing my head, my back, and my shoulders.

The driver seemed determined to hit every road bump. Each time we bounced into a pothole, my head, already aching from a concussion, banged against the hard metal floor. The two troopers in front ignored my painful screams.

Trusting that I was on my way to the emergency room, I prayed I would reach the hospital before the ride finished what the accident started. A few minutes later, my prayers were dashed like a champagne glass tossed ceremoniously into a fireplace.

Despite my injuries, the two deputies dragged me into the Norfolk County police station. They placed me on a hard wooden bench in a holding cell. Slamming the steel door, they walked away laughing, patting each other's backs for a good evening's work.

I remember lying there moaning and spitting up blood. Feeling certain I was about to die in that cold gray concrete bunker, I called out for help over and over.

It wasn't until the precinct's desk sergeant heard my wailing from the holding area and came back to check on the commotion.

The sergeant recognized my plight. He snapped at the patrol officers. "What the hell is wrong with you guys? I don't want this guy dying in my cell. Get him to the hospital ASAP."

The deputy who brought me in shrugged his shoulders and replied, "He looked like he was drunk. I thought he was faking an injury."

The prospect of another ride in that police wagon terrified me. Another trip like the last one would surely bring my death. Yet, I didn't want to die in that police station. With blood spewing from my mouth, I whimpered. "Please help me."

The sergeant barked out. "Call an ambulance; NOW!" Another deputy standing nearby called out with his radio to a nearby fire station. "We need transport to the hospital. Prisoner has injured himself."

After what felt like hours, a fire department ambulance crew lifted me onto a gurney.

"Sir, we are taking you to Norfolk County Medical Center Hospital. It is about ten minutes away." The tone of his voice sounded as if he were asking permission.

"Okay," I mumbled. "What choice do I have?" I thought.

The ambulance ride was better than the police van. At least they strapped me to the gurney, and I wasn't alone. One of the crew members joined me in the back to monitor my condition.

My brains were like scrambled eggs. I still didn't know if Jessica was alive, dead, or somewhere in between. I asked myself, "How did I get so deeply involved in such a dangerous series of events?"

Something had happened that Jessica wasn't telling me. The only thing I knew for sure was the story I would tell the police. Getting it right was my only hope.

Minutes after arriving at the hospital, I found myself surrounded by a group of young men and women in green, blue, and gray hospital scrubs. Thank God, I survived and reached the safety of the hospital emergency room.

The team of healthcare workers pulled and prodded at my clothes as they examined my body for injury. Each time they tore away a garment, I screamed in agony. Between questions like, "Where does it hurt?" and "Sir, can you move your toes?", I drifted in and out of consciousness.

While one attendant took my vital signs, another bundled what was left of my clothes into a large plastic bag. Still, another comforted me by reassuring me, "You're going to be all right."

As I lay there moaning, a young-looking female Emergency Room doctor pulled back my eyelids and flashed an otoscope into each eye. She evaluated me for reaction and to see if I showed any signs of brain damage.

I remembered only days earlier; Jessica once again coerced me into a situation that turned my mundane life upside down.

From our high school days, Jessica controlled everything I did. She had captured my heart and governed my brain. To her I was a puppet dangling on strings she tugged whenever she felt the need. Lying there on an emergency room examination table, I promised myself that if I survived this time, I would cut those strings.

"Can you tell me your name, sir?" asked the doctor.

"Bōdyē," I mumbled.

"You've sustained several injuries. We're going to take X-rays to determine the extent of the damage."

All I could say was, "It hurts. Help me."

The doctor instructed the nurse. "Start a propofol drip, two milligrams, and plasma, two units."

"Yes, doctor," she replied.

In seconds, a young female nurse inserted a hypodermic needle into my hand. I watched as the nurse secured the appliance to my hand with adhesive tape and then strung two clear surgical tubes out of sight from my peripheral vision.

The doctor continued, "We are going to sedate you, Mr. Bōdyē. It will help with the pain. Hang in there. We'll have you back on your feet in no time."

Her optimism did little to bolster my confidence. The pain, both physical and mental, inundated me completely. All I could do was mutter my acceptance, "Okay."

The fast-acting sedative did its job and in seconds, I felt myself falling into a deep sleep. The last thing I remember was seeing Jessica's beautiful face wearing that same smile she wore the day I asked her to the junior prom. They say when you die, your life flashes before you. I prayed this wasn't the beginning of the end.

In the next couple of days, the police will try to piece together the series of events that occurred today. Based on the evidence at hand, they will arrive at a single conclusion. With no other witnesses, the police will rely on Jessica and my recollection of the events leading to the crash.

I knew this much. If we both survived, one of us would go to jail. Which one would the police believe?

* * *

Any outside observer might think this is the beginning and end of my story. It isn't. To fully comprehend my tale of mystery and woe, you must travel back with me in time. As I bring you forward from the beginning, you will better understand my story.

ABLE BODY – PRIVATE INVESTIGATOR

I remember the first day in my new office. I sat at my big wooden desk, staring out the window, thinking about how I arrived at this point in my life.

The brand-new sign on the office door is an eye-catcher. Stenciled in bold burgundy letters shadowed in gold leaf trim, the sign reads, ABLE BODY – Your Undercover Brother. A similar one hangs near the commuter train station's entrance, opposite my office. A busy car wash nearby will soon display a third sign for hundreds of customers every day. Next week: I'll add a fourth sign to a strip mall on the far side of town. It's my first attempt at a marketing plan for my services in such a bold manner and presentation.

Experts I have spoken to tell me the name Able Body is a spoonerism. That, by definition, is the mispronunciation of a name or word with comedic results. That's because the name on my birth certificate clearly states my proper name is "Ābel Bōdyē". It's an Eastern European spelling that no one seems to pronounce correctly.

I let the abuse of my name stand because I've learned that for anyone who reads my name in print, no matter how I emphasize the punctuation, the words ABLE BODY register in their brain.

A consumer focus group I commissioned found that people viewing my advertisements for the first time stated their impression was positive. "What a fun name for a private detective," they thought.

Most people who read my signs will chuckle. Others will comment or even laugh, thinking it's a joke. It doesn't matter if they laugh or not. Overwhelmingly, they remember the name Able Body.

Then, after a few seconds, their thought train changes. They think. "Who wouldn't want to hire an able-bodied detective?" Which is exactly what I want to happen. I want people to remember my sign and, by extension, my name.

After the humor wears off and they safely store my name in their memory bank, their mind fills with other thoughts on the name Able Body. "This cannot be his real name. Who in their right mind would name their child Able Body? Was this some sick joke perpetrated on him at birth?"

Looking at my sign, they can only imagine the number of jokes a boy named Able Body would have to endure growing up.

THE NAME GAME

No, it wasn't a sick joke. My parents, Leonadis and Eisley Bōdyē were clueless immigrants from Bohemia whose goal was to become as American as baseball and apple pie. So, they settled into our new home, a small brick bungalow in Berwyn, Illinois, U.S.A., one of the lower middle-class suburbs that ringed the City of Chicago.

Berwyn, an older bedroom community, even today, consists mostly of classic Chicago brick bungalows and quaint Georgian-style homes. Because of its proximity to Chicago's factories and its inexpensive housing, Berwyn became a magnet for pilgrims from Eastern Europe after the collapse of the Iron Curtain in the 1980s.

Like so many other immigrants searching for a better life, my father, Leonadis, shortened his name to Leon. My mom, Eisley, became Elie. They wanted their only son to have an American-sounding name, so my name, Ābel Bōdyē, became Able Body.

They never understood why everyone else thought the name Able Body was so humorous. To them, it was a good name.

Ever since first grade, I've dreaded the moment of taking attendance in school. No matter the teacher, no matter the class, when the teacher called my name, it was always "Able Body" whose name was called out. On the playground, the parents of my childhood friends would snicker whenever one of the other kids brought my name up in conversation.

As I grew older, I tried to make people call me "Ā Bel", stressing the first syllable. When someone asked me my last name, I always emphasized the "o" and "e" in my last name as long vowels, so it sounded like "BŌ-dyĒ". Pronouncing it phonetically, as "Ā Bel BŌ-dyĒ", didn't make me sound like a cliche.

Despite my best efforts to encourage people to pronounce my name correctly, it didn't work. Through my early years in primary school, then later when I took part in organized sports, whenever the coach called a play or the announcer called the play-by-play, it was always "Able Body" that came out of their mouth. And, as always, I could hear the snickers and giggles following from the opposing players or the crowd of fans in the stadium.

They fill modern psychology books with studies on how the mispronunciation of a person's name affects their psychological well-being. Most conclude it is harmful, often causing bitterness and insecurity.

The results of those studies must never have made it to Berwyn, Illinois. We didn't study philosophers and reference psychologists where I grew up. We just compared ourselves to regular people.

So instead of becoming neurotic, I learned to use the moniker to my advantage. As I matured, it became apparent that people remembered my easy name more often than an ethnic name that was hard to pronounce, like Janko Wiczcoriz or Agnija Skesnick. The zeal of my parents to Americanize my name worked in my favor.

Then, when I started taking an interest in girls, it made introducing myself to them easier. If I met a new girl that I liked, I made it a point to let her know if she needed an able-bodied man, I was right there, at her disposal. My display of confidence made them laugh. That small opening gave me a chance to turn on the charm. Soon the girl was like putty in my hands.

* * *

So, there you have it, an abbreviated version of my life story. That's the way it was growing up in Berwyn, Illinois. Repeating how I grew up makes it all seem so simple compared to today. Most often, it was simple, but there were also times when it was complicated.

Many of the problems I face today started back in high school when I met the girl of my dreams. That girl's name was Jessica Belle Sekelsky.

Because, by the time I reached my senior year, everyone in school knew and liked Able Body. During those years, I was a total jock. I was captain of the baseball team, the star point guard for my school's championship basketball team, and the anchor of our track team's four-man relay squad. The young man everyone knew as Able Body, was tall, handsome, and confident in my three-sport letterman's jacket.

With long wavy hair, bright eyes, and a lean muscular build, Able Body went from being a cliché to mister popularity. Many of the less accomplished students oozed with jealousy. It seemed I had everything a young man needed to succeed in life. As the school's most popular boy, I had my pick of any girl. There was only one girl I wanted. I recognized her right away when she transferred from another high school on the opposite side of town.

It was Jessica, that sweet, petite, dark-haired girl with eyes that sparkled like diamonds on a jewelry store counter, who captured my heart. For me, there was never any doubt. I was sure she was the one.

Jessica, whose good looks and charming personality stood out above the other girls, meant she too had her choice of any beau in the school. She wanted to be with the most popular boy in school, and since that was me, it was a match made in heaven. From the moment we met, it was a whirlwind romance.

We had our first kiss behind the bleachers after my championship basketball game. She wore my letterman's jacket to every game, watching as her hero set school records for home runs, three-point baskets, and record times on the track. We consummated our love in the back seat of my father's Chevy Malibu at the Cook County Forest Preserve near our houses. She was my first.

I remember how it was. We were inseparable. I would have made this beautiful young woman my wife the day after graduation. Jessica Sekelsky would become Jessica Bōdyē. Then, we would spend the rest of our days doing whatever we could to make each other happy. A home with a white picket fence, two children, a dog, a cat, and just like our parents, a simple happy life.

But Jessica had other ideas. She had bigger designs for life after high school. Her plan was an education at a notable college, a high-paying job, and a lifestyle commensurate with financial success. She was going grand, choosing to seek the lifestyle of the rich and famous. She loved me, but my vision wasn't big enough. However, if I wished to join her, she welcomed me to come along.

From my early days in high school, I planned to become an engineer, a Mechanical Engineer to be exact. It made sense. I liked working with my hands and was good with mechanical things. I liked cars and motorcycles and all forms of technical equipment. My dad was a Mechanical Engineer. I wanted to believe I had inherited my father's logical brain. I imagined myself registering patent after patent in the name of Ābel Bōdyē.

An engineer is a good job, one that pays well, and it provides you with a title you can spout with pride as you introduce yourself to a new neighbor. Once I became renowned, the spoonerism "Able Body" would become a thing of the past.

Surely Jessica, aspiring to be a woman of stature, would proudly embrace the role of a successful engineer's wife.

There was only one flaw with my plan to be an engineer. I hated math. I loathed calculus, trigonometry, and complex calculations of all sorts. It turns out I hadn't inherited my father's logical brain. Instead, my talents came from my mother's side of the family. She had other gifts, the type that creative people display. She played a variety of musical instruments, including piano, harp, and cello. A soprano singer with a voice like a songbird, she led the church choir on Sunday mornings. In her later years, she became an accomplished artist. What's more, she had people skills. Everyone in town loved Elie Bōdyē.

Like my mom, I play musical instruments, the piano and the guitar. Making connections with people always came easily for me. It was something I attributed to my success in sports. If you let me, I will talk your ear off about football. Surely, my outgoing personality traits would be a benefit later in life.

Through four years at the University of Illinois, Chicago, Jessica and I remained as close as two people could without becoming one. We commuted to campus, only a few miles from our homes, daily. We hung out in the student union. Together, we attended all the parties as boyfriend and girlfriend.

I had already made my plan, so entering college as a freshman, I chose to pursue an engineering major. Despite my love of all things technical, it wasn't easy for me. I struggled through my undergraduate math courses. With the help of an inexpensive campus tutoring group, my grade point average remained above the level I needed to gain acceptance into graduate school at a university near Chicago renowned for its engineering curriculum. It took a lot of hard work. Meanwhile, I prepared myself for the world of mechanical engineering.

In her first three years, Jessica breezed through her pre-requisites, then in her third year, she applied for a pre-law major and began her pre-law classes.

Fully expecting my romance with Jessica to continue after graduation, I did my best to convince her to apply to the same graduate university in Illinois that I planned to attend for my master's degree. We could stay close to home in the suburbs of Chicago. While we planned our future.

Jessica had other ideas. She made her mind up. She was going to law school in the east, Boston, Massachusetts, to be exact. When she refused to budge on her choice for graduate school, I knew I had to make a choice. Like anyone in love, my choice was simple. Rather than lose Jessica, my plans would simply change.

Since my undergraduate experience showed that math wasn't my strong suit, I rationalized that I wouldn't make a successful engineer. I looked for other options. I enjoyed reading and my talent for dealing with people helped me justify the idea that I might also make an excellent attorney.

Jessica was going to be an attorney. She was going to Boston. I loved Jessica. Nothing else mattered. If she wouldn't change her plans, I would change mine.

In my final year of undergraduate school, I made the abrupt change from a major in engineering to a Bachelor of Arts in Business Administration. My thinking was that acceptance into law school would come more easily with a business degree than a technical degree. The Business Administration curriculum dovetailed best with the prerequisite math and science courses I had already taken. The change increased my workload in the final year more than I wanted because it required me to take extra classes to qualify for the business degree. I had less free time for non-academic activities, but it was my only choice, without staying an extra semester. Despite the extra classes, my desire to be with Jessica kept me on the straight and narrow.

As we grew closer to graduation, Jessica and I both applied to several law schools in the Boston, Massachusetts area. Jessica, who had worked an internship in her last year at a law firm in Chicago, got accepted to Northeastern University. For her, it was a slam dunk. Barring any unforeseen problems, in three years, Jessica was going to become a lawyer.

JESSICA HAS BIGGER PLANS

My story unfolded differently. The last-minute change to my major came back to haunt me. My additional class load in my last year did not allow me time to intern at a law firm. My graduate university application was lacking practical experience. Without experience, other better-qualified candidates stood ahead of me for acceptance. Instead, I found myself wait-listed at Northeastern for their first semester. I waited and hoped for another applicant to drop out, opening a spot for me.

All summer, I remained hopeful that I would still start classes in law school in September of that year. Then another problem arose. Because I hadn't gained acceptance in time for the fall semester, I couldn't get into student housing. I had nowhere to live. The simple solution was to convince Jessica to share an off-campus apartment, but her parents, the Sekelskys, would have none of it. They were old-fashioned, and since they were paying Jessica's rent, they set the rules. Jessica moved into student housing reserved for graduate students. I found an inexpensive room in a boarding house near the university campus just a mile from Jessica's student housing.

The September semester started without me. I considered sitting in on classes to keep pace with Jessica, but missing the first semester of graded classes put me behind schedule to finish in the same graduating class as Jessica. Things were not working as planned. Every day, Jessica went to class and drew closer to becoming a lawyer. Meanwhile, I went looking for something else to do with my time.

RALPH DOWDEN – PRIVATE INVESTIGATOR

While I waited to get accepted into law school with Jessica, I looked for part-time work to supplement my bank account. Waiting tables or stocking shelves didn't appeal to me. I needed something that would enhance my resume. Something with more professional attributes that would dovetail with a law degree. I applied, but the law firms in the City of Boston had no part-time openings. Frustrated, I scoured the internet job boards for anything. Even in the far-out Boston suburbs, no law firms had any vacancies. Then, I stumbled across a position doing computer research for a Private Investigator named Ralph Dowden. It seemed to offer an allusion to legal work. Dowden's office was in Natick, MA, a suburb about twenty miles from Jessica's campus.

Dowden, a former fraud investigator for a large insurance company, specialized in uncovering financial misconduct.

I contacted him and met him at his office for an interview. A man of average size and build, Ralph had a no-nonsense quality. I don't recall ever hearing Ralph laugh. When he asked you a question, you answered promptly. Now in his sixties, Ralph had recently retired from his insurance company with a pension. He tried retirement for a year but couldn't cut the cord.

Ralph, like many people who retired early, didn't have any hobbies. He didn't enjoy traveling. And his job investigating criminals didn't leave him with many personal relationships. Despite this, he had numerous business contacts and a reputation for getting things done. Since retirement did not fit his personality,

Ralph saw this time of his life as an opportunity to be his own boss. He took his experience and knowledge and started an independent investigative agency. His new clients were estate lawyers, insurance companies, and investment firms. They hired him to investigate people whom they suspected were embezzlers, had stolen from their spouses and family members, or were committing other forms of insurance fraud.

One point of emphasis I made when joining Ralph, my new employer, was the job was temporary. Continuing to gain acceptance into law school and my future with Jessica were the two predominant goals in my mind. It was just a matter of time before I achieved success in both arenas. To avoid commuting twenty miles to work every day, I moved out of the rooming house near campus and found an inexpensive apartment outside of town, closer to Dowden's office. I planned to crash there during the week and drive back to campus to visit Jessica on weekends.

At first, the work was simple. The job consisted of looking up people on the computer in Ralph's office. Ralph gave me the names and addresses of the people he was investigating. I searched for more details, like social media accounts, relationship data, or travel logs. As I became more proficient, I learned to expand my searches to gather financial data and criminal history. Ralph had contacts in the legal professions and the police who helped him skirt the rules regarding privacy laws. Within a few weeks, I could collect more information about a person than the person knew about themselves.

It was clean, nine-to-five, work. Then, one Tuesday afternoon, Ralph asked me to do him a favor. He was working on a case that involved monitoring the daily actions of a high-profile executive.

The company that hired him suspected the guy was misappropriating company funds. Ralph always began his investigations with a few days of surveillance. Years of experience told him that understanding the suspects' habits often revealed the reasons they were being investigated. Sometimes they had gambling issues, drug problems, sex addictions, or were having extramarital affairs.

That Tuesday, Ralph's grandson was visiting from out of town. The boy wanted to go to a Boston Red Sox baseball game. Ralph asked me to pinch-hit for him that evening on his surveillance job. He described it as simple. Ralph said, "Just follow him, see where he goes, make some notes on his whereabouts, and snap a few pictures if you see anything suspicious." He offered me a fifty-dollar bonus if I would follow the guy and document his movements.

At first, I resisted. "Ralph, I am not a licensed Private Investigator. What if I get caught?"

"There's nothing illegal about you driving around town behind this guy's car. Follow him and find out where he goes at night. As long as he doesn't notice you or you don't do something stupid like getting a ticket for parking in a no-parking zone, you won't have any trouble. Besides, you're my employee, working for me under my license."

It sounded easy enough. Then Ralph reached into his drawer and pulled out a badge. It wasn't from any police force or security firm I had ever seen before. The badge was a prop. Still, it looked official enough to fool the average person.

"Here, just to be safe, if anyone bothers you, flash this at them. They will back off. Whatever you do, don't let them look too closely at the badge. They will see it's phony. And for heaven's sake, don't show it to the police."

Despite my apprehension, I wasn't doing anything important that evening, and I sure could use an extra fifty dollars.

Ralph had already been following the man for several days. To make sure I followed the right guy, he showed me pictures taken with his camera. On a slip of paper, he wrote the guy's name, home address, and the address of his place of employment. Finally, he jotted down the suspect's automobile make and model and his license plate number.

"He will be at work for a few more hours, so start there." He looked at his watch. "If you leave now, you can get there before he sneaks out."

It seemed like a slam dunk. Shortly after 5:00 p.m., I got in my car and headed over to the offices of Charles, Turner, and Boson, a consulting firm that specialized in helping construction companies obtain zoning approvals and variances for large redevelopment projects. The "pigeon," as Dowden referred to him, was an executive named Walter Koenig.

The firm leased office space in a large, modern office building of steel and glass that was home to several up-and-coming businesses. The exclusive address was a key element in making the impression of being a successful consulting firm. Their location offered a high-profile image that helped the company attract new business.

I perused the parking lot, looking for the dark blue Cadillac Escalade that Ralph identified as Koenig's business car.

Sure enough, right in front of the building, in a spot assigned to AVP Business Development, sat Koenig's Escalade. I found an empty parking spot three rows back that had a direct view of the indigo beast. Pulling into the spot, I pushed my seat back and made sure the battery in my cell phone had a full charge. I grabbed the notepad that Ralph used to log his actions and jotted down the time. Then I did just as Ralph instructed. I sat and waited.

Around 6:30 p.m., Koenig emerged from the front door of the building with his cell phone pressed against his ear. He climbed into the front seat of the blue Escalade, too busy to notice anyone who might be hanging nearby. He did not see me seated in my car watching him. Using my phone's camera. I snapped a picture, noting the time. Seconds later, I watched as his car's backup lights came on and Koenig backed out of his parking spot. He put the car in gear and sped off. I gave Koenig just enough head start not to alarm him, then followed behind him in hot pursuit.

Koenig sped across town until he pulled into the driveway of a beautifully restored Dutch Colonial home in the trendy neighborhood of Brook Farm.

Noting the time and address of the house, I cruised past using my phone to take a picture of the building and car in the driveway. I turned my car around and parked on an incline a few hundred feet uphill from the house. From my perch, I could see the front of the house and Koenig's car in the driveway. Once again, I pushed my seat back and relaxed, waiting for Koenig's next move.

The next activity surprised me. About an hour after Koenig entered the building, a local pizza delivery car pulled up in front of the house. It was Uncle Sal's Pizza, a popular neighborhood restaurant known for its delicious pizza and tasty plates of pasta. In my rush to leave the office, I neglected to bring any food or drink. It was getting late, and I was starving. I couldn't leave my surveillance post. I wondered. "Would it be wrong to order me a pizza and have it delivered here to my car?" After a moment of contemplation, I concluded it was probably too risky.

I took a picture of the delivery car, making sure I caught the license number of the vehicle. Seconds later, a slender young man about twenty years old ran up the steps and rang the doorbell. A beautiful blonde woman, quite a few years younger than Koenig, answered the door. I quickly snapped a picture, as best I could, of her handing the delivery driver cash and then closing the door behind her. I jumped to the conclusion that Koenig and this woman were involved romantically.

Nothing else of notoriety happened until about 11:00 p.m. I was half asleep from boredom when I noticed the front porch light come on at the house I was watching. Koenig stepped out of the front door. He ambled down the steps, cell phone in his hand, and jumped back into his automobile.

Koenig backed his blue chariot out of the driveway onto the street. As expected, he turned and headed back north in the opposite direction he came.

Making sure I went undetected; I followed a safe distance back as our two cars cruised the back roads towards Koenig's house in the western suburb of Waltham. Twenty minutes later, Koenig turned into the driveway of a three-story brick and stone mansion. In the dim light, I could see what looked like a plush manicured lawn and extensive flower beds of white hydrangea and purple lilacs.

Again, noting the time, I watched as Koenig pulled his car around the back of the house and into a massive four-car garage. I watched as the garage door closed and Koenig disappeared into the house. In systematic order, the lights on the main floor flicked on and off. Minutes later, the lights went on, then off, in several of the second-story rooms.

After hanging around for a few more minutes, it became apparent that Koenig had retired for the night. I made my last entries into Ralph's logbook and then headed for home. Tomorrow morning, I will report Koenig's activities to Ralph.

On my way back home, I took a slight detour past the storefront of Uncle Sal's Pizza. I was hoping they were still open, thinking I had time to score a late-night snack. As I pulled up, I noticed the closed sign on the door. Then, I noticed the young pizza delivery driver who delivered the pizza to Koenig's blonde associate still standing out front.

Even though Ralph told me to only follow Koenig, I stopped my car and approached the young man. Flashing the phony badge at the youth with all the bravado of a veteran police officer, I said. "Young man, you delivered a pizza to a house in Brook Farm earlier tonight. What was the name on the order?"

The young man, obviously intimidated, replied, "Bardy, I think?"

"You think? Well, what is it?" I snapped.

"I mean, yes, sir, it was Bardy."

With practically no effort, I learned the name of the woman Koenig was visiting. It would impress Ralph. Because I learned that extra piece of information without any research. Tomorrow, I promised myself I would look up the name Bardy. It might have relevance to Ralph's case.

For no discernable reason, I asked the young man. "What did they order?"

"A large ham and pineapple with barbeque sauce," he replied.

"Seriously?" I said, "Ham and pineapple? A barbeque pizza? What's this world coming to?"

"Sorry, sir. I only deliver."

Frustrated, I asked the kid, "Do you have any leftover orders?"

"No sir," he replied. "We are closed for the night. They cleaned everything up."

Unsure what to do, I handed the young man five dollars and winked at the boy. "We never had this conversation."

"Yes, sir," the young man replied.

I got back in my car and drove off, thinking the poor kid was probably shitting his pants. Or at least confused. Why would a cop give him a five-dollar tip?

I hurried home to my apartment to find something to eat. While I missed out on Uncle Sal's Italian food, at least I could make myself a peanut butter sandwich. Even a peanut butter sandwich is better than a ham and pineapple pizza.

While nothing of any notoriety happened, it was my first foray as a private investigator. I felt excited about performing my first stakeout. I went to sleep that night smiling.

The next morning, I looked up the name Bardy at the address where Koenig spent the evening. It turned out to be his daughter. Nothing as nefarious as I had hoped. Still, I told myself that my work that evening made me a full-fledged Private Investigator. I kept the badge that Ralph gave me as a reminder.

Working part-time for Dowden's agency wasn't what I envisioned when I left Illinois for Massachusetts. The plan was supposed to be to go to graduate school, pass the bar, become a lawyer, and live happily ever after. Somehow, I got detoured. Still, I had Jessica and at least this temp job kept cash in my pocket while I waited for the next semester and an opening in law school, which would be my eventual path to success.

For the first few months of the semester, my relationship with Jessica remained status quo. Jessica went to class during the week, and I put in my hours with Ralph Dowden out in Natick. On the weekends, I stayed with Jessica in her studio apartment. Then Jessica started getting invited to hang out with her classmates. At first, she brought me along to her group meetings and weekend parties, but I didn't feel comfortable with her new friends. I was on the outside. She was in with the in-crowd. Jessica fit in perfectly with the other law students, most of whom were from privileged homes on the East Coast. I wasn't a law student, and I was from the Midwest. That, by extension, made me an outsider.

Then in mid-October, Jessica took up association with a third-year law student named Barry McGleam. Barry grew up in Weston, Massachusetts, the son of a renowned heart surgeon and socialite mother. A spoiled brat who had everything money could buy, he never took no for an answer. Whatever Barry wanted, he found some way or someone to get it for him. Barry wanted Jessica. He didn't care that she belonged to me.

One Friday night, Jessica and I attended a party with her classmates. At the party, Barry and I sparred over Jessica's attention. To my chagrin, Barry was boldly flirting with Jessica right in front of me.

With a stern voice, I reminded Barry that Jessica was with me. I thought the matter was settled until a few minutes later. Barry, ignoring my earlier warning, took Jessica's hand and tried to pull her away to another room. I grabbed Barry's arm, forcing a confrontation.

The altercation escalated into an exchange of blows. That's when being Able Body, the high school athlete, came in handy. In seconds, I had Barry on the floor. With his arm in a hammerlock and my elbow on his neck, I pressed Barry's face deep into the carpet leaving a rug burn on his cheek and neck. It took three other partygoers to separate us and save Barry before he ended up in the hospital.

Barry, in his arrogant nature, threatened to get his revenge through legal action. I took the low road and swore that I would bury him in a shallow grave should he ever start up with Jessica again. From that moment, Barry and I became mortal enemies.

Although Jessica left the party that night with me, she continued her friendship with Barry. Despite my best efforts, my post-graduate experience wasn't going well. I could feel Jessica slipping away from me. Beating Barry to a pulp might make me feel better about myself, but it couldn't save my relationship with Jessica.

Things only got worse from then on. Jessica and I argued often. For me, it was the relationships she formed with the other law students I opposed. A relationship that wasn't involving me.

She felt I was holding her back. She argued that to accomplish her goals, she needed to associate with the right people. People who can pave her path to success.

* * *

Jessica never told me our time together was through. Not in so many words. She kept repeating that her plans were changing. She had dreams. More and more, from the way she talked, it didn't sound like her plans still included me.

Then one day my dreams for a future with the woman I loved disappeared. Barry asked Jessica to move in with him and his roommates in their off-campus house, and she accepted his invitation. She declined to renew the lease on her apartment and instructed me to gather whatever belongings I wanted to keep.

I packed my toothbrush and phone charger and tossed them into my backpack. The handwriting was on the wall. Before the fall semester ended, Jessica and I went our separate ways.

With the chances of marrying Jessica Sekelsky gone, continuing to pursue acceptance into law school became unimportant to me. Being a fancy East Coast lawyer wasn't my dream. It was hers. My dream was to be married to Jessica.

REALITY CALLS AGAIN

By the time the snow started falling on the East Coast, I gave Ralph my two-week notice. After five months in Boston, I returned to my hometown of Berwyn, Illinois, in the suburbs of Chicago, with my tail between my legs. My quest for law school was a bust. I had an undergraduate degree in Business Administration, but no job and a shaky future.

My time in Boston wasn't a total waste. I learned something from working for Ralph Dowden that I never learned growing up in Berwyn. Money makes the world go around. It gave me better insight into the way rich people act and how the wealthy manipulate the law in their favor. Rich people who can afford to hire high-priced lawyers can get away with almost anything.

Ralph had a sign hanging on his office wall that said, "We all deserve justice. Most people can't afford it." If I remembered nothing else from my time in Boston, Dowden's sign would remain as one of the most profound statements that I can recall. My memory of that sign, and what it implied, would return often throughout my lifetime.

After returning home, I looked for a job that dovetailed with my business degree. I would send in my resume, follow up with the hiring manager, and schedule a meeting to discuss my future. If they liked me, I put on a business suit for an interview where I pretended to be everything the company wanted in an employee.

I kept trying my hand at management jobs at the business offices of large corporations in downtown Chicago, hoping to find a good fit. I received several offers for white-collar positions, but they were boring office jobs like staff manager, which in real life meant I would be a paper pusher.

It seemed I was like many other college graduates without a true vocation. My destiny was to work a nine-to-five job. While I could make enough money to support myself, working a job I didn't want would doom me to a humdrum existence, probably for the rest of my life. There had to be more. "But what else was there?" I wondered.

There was one good thing about living in Berwyn, it's an easy commute to downtown Chicago. Renting an apartment in Berwyn is much cheaper compared to apartments in the city or the newer, far-western suburbs. But Berwyn was boring for a young man, so while I waited for my future to unfold, I started hanging out a lot in the trendy up-and-coming neighborhoods ringing Chicago's central business district. During the week, I stayed after work to party, and on weekends, I took the train into town to meet my friends.

When I wasn't hanging out at a bar or attending a sporting event, I spent my quiet hours in Berwyn thinking of Jessica and wondering how her new life in Boston was unfolding. The answer came one day when I was browsing Jessica's social media account. She struck the final blow to my self-esteem. Jessica married Barry McGleam in a lavish ceremony at a prestigious Norfolk country club. The pictures of her smiling happily in a white wedding gown, with Barry at her side, shattered my heart. She was now Jessica Sekelsky-McGleam.

* * *

After bouncing around from job to job for over two years, I hadn't found my niche. I realized that a staff job at a large corporation wasn't the career I wanted for the rest of my life.

A friend I met at a bar on the Northside of Chicago worked in construction at a mid-sized company in town. He told me his employer was looking for an office manager. The role of manager at a construction company sounded like a fitting position for a recent college graduate. As a manager, someone with responsibilities, I could be proud of my work. The idea intrigued me.

I applied and was hired based on the job description, as an office manager. It turned out to be a job ordering supplies. My tasks included buying materials like lumber, metal, concrete, and tools for various construction sites. Despite the impressive job description, I was little more than a glorified clerk.

It was a hard job, both mentally and physically. I not only negotiated the purchases, but I also had to load and deliver the trucks myself. If it was a large quantity, too big for one person, I would meet the supplier at the job site and monitor the delivery. The boss held me responsible for all the construction materials and tools. If the shipment was delayed or they delivered the wrong product, I took the blame.

The company relied on a tight schedule of ordering and on-time delivery to keep the construction workers busy and completing their jobs on time. When the workers couldn't work, the job costs soared. If the job shut down because of procurement, I got the blame.

My boss, the owner of the company, was an unforgiving dictator. He barked out orders to his employees and screamed profanities when things went wrong. After weeks of coming home night after night, exhausted and drained, I walked off the job. No amount of money could make me continue working for him. Once again, I was an unemployed college graduate.

THE ONLY JOB I UNDERSTOOD

Out of work, with bills to pay, I needed to change my approach. Day after day, I spent my mornings sitting in a coffee shop rewriting my resume to match job descriptions for jobs I didn't want. Then, one day, over a cup of cold, dark roast coffee, an epiphany struck. I realized I didn't want to be an employee of some heartless corporation. I was a free spirit and should remain free.

I stumbled across an advertisement on one of the internet job boards for an assistant to a Private Investigator. The job description was not decidedly different from the work I did for my former employer, Ralph Dowden, in Boston.

While the job opening was in Tulsa, Oklahoma, and I had no desire to relocate to Tulsa, the job advertisement gave me an idea. I realized I didn't want to work for someone else, in Chicago, Tulsa, or anywhere. Starting a business of my own was going to be my solution to happiness and success.

After retiring, Ralph Dowden started his own business by contracting with corporate clients and insurance companies to investigate policyholder fraud. He made a lot of money doing it. Ralph rarely got involved in messy situations, and he had control over his own destiny. Even though the people he investigated occasionally threatened him with bodily harm, he would shrug off the threats and move on to the next client.

I remembered the exhilaration I felt doing that first surveillance job for Ralph Dowden. It made me wonder if a business modeled after Dowden's investigative business, right there in my hometown of Berwyn, would be a viable option. After a few minutes of searching on the internet, to my surprise, I discovered my agency would be the only Private Investigator's office in Berwyn, Illinois. If people needed someone to investigate a mystery, my detective agency would be their first and only choice.

A little more research told me that for a minimum investment, I could form a limited liability company, rent office space, and start advertising. I thought I had found my path to success. I just needed a business plan.

With nothing more to lose, I made my decision. I was going to follow in Ralph Dowden's footsteps and become a Private Investigator.

* * *

While there are schools to teach you the business end of becoming a private investigator, developing skills as an effective undercover sleuth is a seat-of-the-pants process. It takes confidence and cunning to hide in plain sight. You learn as you go, gaining experience with each investigation.

I needed more advice than I could get from the internet. I had an enjoyable learning experience in Massachusetts. There was one person I knew who could help me get started in my quest.

I looked in my phone and I still had the phone number of my old boss, Ralph Dowden. Hitting the send button, I listened as the phone started ringing. To my surprise, a voice at the other end answered, "Ralph Dowden here, how can I help you?"

"Mr. Dowden, this is Ābel Bōdyē." By using my proper name, I hoped to demonstrate a tone of professionalism. "I worked for you a couple of years ago. I was the college student who did internet research."

At first, he didn't respond. The silence sounded like Ralph didn't remember me. He had several interns over the years. Too many to remember. Then, after a minute, it clicked in. "Oh yeah, BODY, I remember. How are ya? Did you ever become a lawyer?"

"No, that didn't work out. I never got accepted into law school."

"Too bad. You seemed to have a good head on your shoulders," Ralph commented.

I changed the subject. "I am thinking of starting a Private Investigation business modeled after yours."

I told Ralph about my plan to start my own agency and become an entrepreneur like him.

"Why would you want to do that?" He said, "I thought you were a college guy?"

I replied. "College hasn't helped me much."

"Hey, whatever happened to that pretty girl you were chasing? Seems like you should be talking with her."

"That didn't work out either. She ended up marrying a big-name lawyer in Boston. I'm back living in Berwyn, Illinois, trying to get my feet back on the ground. That's why I called you. I need to know where to begin."

"Hmm..." Ralph paused. "So, you wanna know the secrets of being a successful investigator? Okay, I have three pieces of advice. Here they are. One, stay up late at night, the bad guys always screw up at night. Two, don't feel sorry for anyone. The suspects and the clients. They are all lying. Three, always look over your shoulder."

"What else?" I asked.

"That's about it. You're pretty smart. You will learn as you go."

According to Ralph Dowden, my education was complete. The rest was on me to figure it out.

* * *

Ralph's three pieces of advice weren't as helpful as I hoped. I guessed that Ralph had been in the business too long to remember how he started and where he developed his expertise. I lost a little faith in Ralph that day. Maybe he should retire?

Disheartened, I realized, I was on my own.

I researched *private investigators' licenses* on the internet. Within seconds, ads for licensing schools flooded my screen. I learned the first step to licensing is attending a series of training classes that total twenty hours. Twenty hours seemed pretty easy. Amongst the ads, I found a school that offered affordable online classes. It seemed so simple. In a week, I could start digging into other people's lives and make money doing it.

That is when I hit my first roadblock. My conversation with Ralph led me to believe entry to the private investigator business was a slam dunk. Anyone can do it. Throw up a shingle, answer the phone, and go undercover. That may be true in Massachusetts, where you can obtain your license without a waiting period. However, meeting the requirements in Illinois for becoming a private investigator takes longer. Illinois requires a three-year apprenticeship at a licensed agency. Then you can apply for your license.

It meant starting at the bottom as an assistant. Assistants are in high demand at larger agencies. They give them the crappiest assignments like late-night surveillance, posing as a patsy for some shyster, or even dumpster diving, for evidence. Like my stint with Ralph Dowden, most assistants only work for a short time. They lose interest and find a better job.

I had no choice. Staying in Illinois required a three-year apprenticeship. Not wanting to relocate back to the Boston area, I needed to get started on pursuing a license in Illinois.

My qualifications were meek, so I called Ralph back and asked if I could use his name as a reference. Despite not remembering me, he agreed. I rewrote my resume to match the job descriptions I found online and then applied for a full-time position with several agencies.

I emphasized my strong points, such as my computer skills and my experience with research work at Ralph Dowden's agency. Stressing my computer skills would be the best way to ensure I get a computer research position. I wanted to avoid any position that required me to dig through bags of garbage or follow unsavory characters down dark alleys. Several agencies offered me a starting position as a research analyst.

I chose a position with M.I.A. and More, an agency on the Southside of Chicago that specializes in searching for missing people. The largest investigative agency in Chicago, M.I.A. and More, had two offices, the main office in the city and a second in the suburbs. The in-town office worked best for me. Employing eight licensed investigators and fourteen research assistants, the office looked more like a modern call center than a dark, smoky noir-imaged private detective like you see in the movies.

It wasn't exactly the deep dark crime-solving scenarios people think of when they hire a detective. A lot of it was finding missing heirs or reconnecting broken families. Still, several of the people we searched for were dead. They died for various reasons from illness to old age. Only one missing person I researched had met with a violent death, shot by an unknown assassin. Thinking they might want to add my evidence to their investigation, I reported my findings to the local police. I was helping follow up on a crime. The police had closed the case years earlier. I don't think they really cared about my new evidence any longer. At least I did my part to help the victim and his family get closure.

My time with M.I.A. and More went faster than expected. Their training classes were excellent. I learned a lot about the best tools used to find hidden information about people. I also received a lot of practical advice from the experienced detectives who worked there. They taught me the valuable skill of being involved in the action while somehow remaining invisible during investigations.

I counted down the days until I could apply for my license. Including the five months I collaborated with Ralph Dowden. During that time, I took more classes and formulated a business and marketing plan so that I could hit the ground running.

Thirty-one months to the day of signing on with M.I.A. and More, I handed in my resignation. My boss, the owner of the company, was sorry to see me go. He offered me a position as a detective, which I declined. He wished me luck, then reminded me I was welcome to return if things didn't work out on my own.

Smiling cautiously, he repeated, "This is a tough business to break into."

I thanked him.

My hard work paid off. I had met the legal requirements to form a self-employed agency.

I had a crazy idea of how to attract customers. My agency needed a catchy name and slogan. I knew it was tacky, but my name, the nemesis of my childhood days, Able Body, would be my trademark. So, despite the advice from my friends and family, the *Able Body – Your Undercover Brother*, detective agency became a reality. The name was whimsical, but I was serious. Only one question remained; would other people take me seriously?

BERWYN'S ONLY DETECTIVE AGENCY

I used my time at M.I.A. and More to learn the business. With the help of my former colleagues, I worked up a detailed business plan to guide my operation. Finding an office for my day-to-day activities was my first task. I found a small office in Berwyn's Depot District, a central business locality, which would meet my needs. I had seen the building across from the train station on my daily commute into downtown Chicago.

Despite not being an obvious choice for starting a business, Berwyn's affordable rent made it an appealing option.

Besides being a sleepy, established suburb of Chicago, comprising apartment homes and brick bungalows. Berwyn is also a commuter hub for business executives traveling into and out from downtown Chicago. A dozen or more packed commuter trains from the rich western suburbs pass by the location daily. So, every day, hundreds of people pass this office building on their way to work. I convinced myself that every cheating husband and insecure wife in the Western suburbs would see my sign from their seat on the train. Sooner or later, as they pondered their situation, they would hire me to investigate their spouse or partner.

Unlike other downtrodden neighborhoods surrounding the city, the community was on the upturn. Berwyn was old, but not seedy. The city center was a prime location for urban renewal. The building I chose was a typical two-story walkup with a flower shop and dry cleaner sharing the first-floor retail space. Upstairs, the building's owner, a man named Valter Zermenski, a Hungarian immigrant, maintained business offices. Zermenski ran a thriving mortgage brokerage on one side and a prosperous title insurance company on the other side of the building. His two businesses served the Berwyn real estate market for over twenty years. When new government regulations changed the mortgage business, Zermenski found it hard to compete with the big banks and online lenders. Younger people no longer wanted to sit down with the neighborhood mortgage broker. They just go online and fill out a mortgage application. The computer will review their financial data and approve or deny their application. It saves time and money.

Nearing retirement age, Zermenski, shut down the mortgage business but kept the more lucrative title insurance agency going for a few more years.

The old building, to this day, has an air of mystery, reminiscent of the roaring twenties. Built with salmon-colored Chicago brick and a stone facade that gave it an aura of elegance and a classic appeal.

The fired clay bricks on the exterior have since weathered into an earthy pink. Except, years of tuck-pointing with different-colored mortars left the walls a patchwork of shades. The number of repairs left you asking, how much longer the building would remain upright before it collapses under its own weight? Despite its age, the old building still maintained much of its original charm.

The windowsills were all cut from original sandstone, and the architectural design of the window frames used a dark wood accent. From the ground below, the view through the cloudy upstairs windows gave a glow like a yellow halo, adding to the mystery. When you stood on the street and looked up, it appeared as if Phillip

Marlowe himself was running his storied detective agency from the upstairs offices.

Inside the second-floor office space, Zermenski maintained the old post-war-style interior. It had rich-looking walls featuring floor-to-ceiling dark walnut wood paneling. The metal doorknobs, hinges, heat registers, and other accents were all polished brass. The still shiny hardwood floors were aged to a golden patina. and creaked ever so obligingly when you moved too quickly across the room.

Mr. Zermenski took an immediate liking to me because I grew up in Berwyn and had Bohemian ancestry. He made the unused office space available to me for a reasonable rent. The best part was that he leased me the space fully furnished with two desks, two large leather office chairs, and several filing cabinets. A commercial phone system was already in place, and the building provided Wi-Fi internet access. The inner office, the one I would use as my exclusive client meeting room, had a private bathroom. All I needed was to supply my new telephone number and my own computers, and I was in business.

Zermenski and I smiled, shook hands, negotiated a month-to-month lease, and I was ready to put my sign on the door. I went to an office supply store and bought paper, pens, manila folders, and one of those big desk calendars. The type you can make notes on when a notepad isn't handy. I also bought a large whiteboard and dry-erase marker pens, the kind you see television detectives use to plot out complex cases.

To save money, I stopped by the local thrift shop and found a used single-serve pod coffee maker, a small under-the-counter refrigerator, and a digital clock. I hung the clock on the wall above the door where I could see it from my desk. That clock was the best investment I made. Whenever I answered a phone call, or someone entered the room, a quick glance at the digital display told me the exact time of the event.

While at that same thrift store, I fell in love with a framed picture of a man and woman cloaked in darkness. The picture symbolized the cloak-and-dagger theme I wanted to portray for my business. It went on the wall next to my desk.

Across the room, tucked against the back wall, I placed a brown leather couch that Zermenski no longer needed for his mortgage business. It would soon become my place of refuge. I spend many a late night or early morning asleep on that couch. More than once, I spent an amorous hour or two on that couch with a client who couldn't pay her bill but offered to take it out in trade. It wasn't good business, but it was the reality of my life.

Behind my huge wooden desk, a large picture window offered me a clear view of the commuter train station and the busy shopping district on the streets below that surrounded the train depot.

As I watched the people come and go, I sat contemplating why people do the sort of things that make them need a private investigator. Getting into their heads helps me understand their side of whatever shady situation they were involved in.

A few days after shaking hands with my new landlord, Valter Zermenski, I hung my license on the wall and was sitting proudly at my desk, surveying all that was mine. It wasn't much, but it was a start. Now all I had to do was wait for the phone to ring.

* * *

The impression people have of Private Investigators is they make a living following wayward husbands and appeasing frustrated wives. That idea is only partly true. Yes, I am at times a snoop but performing challenging investigations for business clients was the long-term goal. I knew it would take me a while to build my business and claim a professional image. For those first few weeks in business, attracting clients was challenging. In the beginning, most of my jobs were limited to surveillance and taking pictures. I wasn't savvy enough to know which of the pictures might or might not display incriminating evidence.

When people are paying you, it's important to take their needs seriously. Despite their sometimes kooky requests, I took them seriously and did a good job. But doing a good job and claiming expertise alone isn't sufficient to generate the income I needed to survive. I quickly realized I needed better name recognition. I wanted people to think of me first when they needed help.

Signs alone won't bring in enough new business. I hired a local marketing company to produce a series of YouTube videos starring me as Your Undercover Brother, a character they invented to show my creative side. The gambit worked. People remembered *Able Body–Your Undercover Brother*, and soon my phone started ringing with greater regularity. Most of the calls weren't from serious clients, but I was getting noticed. It showed we were going in the right direction.

My childhood foil, the mispronunciation of my name, Able Body, was paying dividends later in life.

Being the new business in town, I needed a niche. I advertised my computer research skills as a specialty that other private investigators might not have. Then I added an extra benefit. I didn't just target the unfaithful spouse; I researched the unfaithful spouse's new lover. The strategy was to give the partner who hired me greater leverage when and if their divorce lawyers got into negotiations. It was an added value that a lot of other private investigators didn't provide. I did such a good job of digging up dirt that several of the prominent divorce lawyers in the Chicago area began hiring me to bolster their clients' cases, even if they had no prior evidence of cheating.

Still, it was obvious to me I wouldn't make a decent living if my only business was following cheating spouses around. To earn extra money in the weeks when I had no clients, I took a few jobs providing personal security for big-name celebrities at private events. My private investigator's license and my insurance doesn't authorize me to do personal security. Most people assume a detective is a tough guy who can provide for their safety. It was a risk I probably should not have taken, but I needed the money, so I took the chance.

I expanded my business by learning to offer advanced services, like in-depth reports, preparing affidavits, and coaching clients for their depositions. Not only did it increase the size of my invoices, but I also became known as an expert who helped his clients sort out their problems. Little by little, my business and name recognition grew.

Sometimes people hired me to investigate bad guys. The type that doesn't take kindly to having their unscrupulous activities investigated. It added an element of risk. If the bad guys caught me being a spy, my safety would be in danger. If someone blew my cover, the entire investigation would go up in smoke. Then I could say goodbye to my big paycheck. If it happened too often, I could say goodbye to my excellent reputation.

I worked hard to grow my business, to be more like the agency of my previous employer, Ralph Dowden. I wanted to get into the insurance fraud business. Ralph taught me that working with large corporations that have deep pockets is the only way to ensure a steady income stream.

About a year into establishing my reputation, I took a job investigating a business owner who used a couple of small businesses to launder money for a gambling ring he ran in the city.

As part of that investigation, I posed as a banker with a gambling problem. The ruse was going smoothly until I asked too many questions about his business. The bookie grew suspicious and turned the tables on me. He had two thugs follow me around. When they discovered I wasn't who I pretended to be, they dragged me from my car. Tied me up, duct taped my mouth shut, then drove me out of town to an isolated forest preserve where they beat the hell out of me. They left me in a dark wooded area bloody and bruised. I crawled out of the brush onto a dirt road where a forest preserve ranger found me and called for help.

It was a lesson I learned the hard way. The deeper you become involved in a case, the greater the risk. After that, I learned to be smarter, and I started carrying a gun.

I had limited knowledge about guns, but I strongly disliked being beaten and left for dead. The first gun I purchased was a .44 Magnum. I saw it in one of those badass, blow-the-guy-away cop movies and decided that was what I needed. I visualized myself as a tough guy, and the pretty blonde sales lady at the gun store made the sale by convincing me that women like men with big, powerful pieces.

After a few hours of practicing at a local gun range, I realized how impractical the Magnum was. That gun could blast someone or something into oblivion. Every time I shot at a target; it would explode beyond recognition. But the big gun was difficult to carry and impossible to conceal. I knew I needed something more practical, a defensive weapon. My second gun was a .25 caliber Beretta. Despite its limited stopping power, the Beretta is capable of intimidating most would-be attackers. Plus, I could carry it easily in a holster under my jacket or behind my back, tucked into a belt.

Despite my distaste for the use of lethal weapons, I used the Beretta to get myself out of a jam on more than one occasion.

MY RIGHT HAND WOMAN

The entrance to my second-floor offices is a doorway at street level, right between the dry cleaners and the florist. Customers enter the wood-framed glass door and then ascend a flight of stairs to a common reception area. To the right of the staircase are the offices of Mr. Zermenski's title company. Turn to the left and you'll find my private office door.

The reception area has room for two desks, a couch, and several chairs. One desk and several filing cabinets were being used for Zermenski's business. The other was available for my new agency. Before I moved in, the receptionist, Thelma Jenkins, handled secretarial services for both Zermenski's mortgage business and the title company.

When both of Zermenski's businesses were flourishing, he had enough work to keep Thelma busy, but when his mortgage business shut down, there wasn't enough to fill her workday. So, along with paying my monthly rent, I agreed to pay half of Thelma's salary. In exchange, she would answer my phones, schedule my appointments, and do some filing when I was out of the office. The arrangement worked out as a win-win situation for me and Zermenski.

Thelma, a full-figured black woman in her mid-forties, had the perfect personality for her job. She multi-tasks with the best of them, keeping track of appointments, paperwork, and client information. Thelma always made the occasional walk-in customer feel welcome. During busy appointment days, she brought donuts and pastries for the office waiting areas.

A single mother, with two teenage boys, Thelma handled crises as calmly and coolly as anyone I ever met. It didn't matter if Zermenski had a real estate deal that failed to close on time or if the wife of a cheating business executive was having an anxiety attack. Thelma was always calm, cool, and ready with a kind word or a simple solution to a complex problem.

She wasn't a raving beauty, but Thelma still had some alluring qualities. She had a bright smile that was accented by her ebony skin, and despite her easy-going disposition, Thelma was a strong woman. I appreciate strong women. Strong women make me feel secure and, much as I hate to admit it, they turn me on.

My mom taught me behind every successful man is a strong woman with bills to pay. That was the situation between me and Thelma Jenkins. I worked a lot of oddball hours. Much of my surveillance work occurred in the evening or late-night hours. Thelma became the daytime face of Able Body – Your Undercover Brother.

When I first moved back to Illinois, I spent a lot of time in downtown Chicago with the party crowd. Since opening this agency, I no longer had time for partying. Conversely, my dating calendar has gone begging. Thelma was pretty much the only woman I interacted with regularly.

Sometimes I would sit at my desk and watch Thelma walk across the room. Her ample but shapely buttocks always caught my eye. Like all men my age, I get lonely sometimes. When I was alone, I fantasized about how Thelma and I might be together. There were days when I wanted to invite her to join me on the couch in my office. As a single mother, without a man in her life, she probably feels the same loneliness.

Despite my deviant mind, I realized getting romantically involved with Thelma was probably not the best idea. Finding a good receptionist and secretary is much harder than finding a female companion.

* * *

About a year after my agency opened for business, I was building a reputation as a solid choice for undercover work. Things were going well, and I started paying my bills on time. Then something unexpected happened. My landlord, Mr. Zermenski, had a stroke. The stroke left him partially disabled, but he insisted it was just a matter of time until he regained his health and could return to his title insurance business. While months of physical therapy helped him regain his range of motion, he lacked the energy to reopen his office. In less than two years, my investigative agency was the sole occupant of the upstairs offices.

When Zermenski shuttered the title insurance business, I was all Thelma had left to worry about. If she wanted to keep her job, she had to make sure I made enough money to pay her salary. She took on additional tasks of marketing and sales of my investigative services to anyone in need of an undercover partner. Much to my surprise, my business improved. Thelma became better at bringing in new business than me.

Since Thelma had the administrative tasks in order, I realized I could spend more of my working hours away from the office. I was asking more of Thelma, and she willingly took on more and more responsibilities. Thelma even took some online computer classes to improve her research skills. She didn't have the title, but she became my de facto partner. I laughingly referred to her as my Undercover Sister.

We worked as a team. I still did all the actual digging work. Thelma always made sure I was digging in the right place.

The agency's first big money break came exactly twenty-three months after I hung my shingle out in front of the old brick building. Business was slow that week, and I was looking into the case of a resident who claimed her neighbor was poisoning her dogs. The police weren't taking her seriously, so she hired me. People will spend any amount of money to protect their pets. I gave her a discount because I needed the work.

At that point, I still hadn't developed the street smarts that a lot of experienced detectives display, but I was working hard. The more I worked, the more I became known as an investigator who could uncover secret plans by dishonest characters. My computer research skills were better than most gumshoes. Most detectives follow people around and wait for them to screw up. The experience I had working at M.I.A. and More taught me how to dig into people's digital footprints, meaning I didn't always have to get in the car and follow them around.

One afternoon, I called into the office to ask Thelma if anything unusual was happening.

Thelma rarely gets animated, but that day, excitement filled her voice. She had never sounded so chirpy to me, talking a mile a minute. A big-name insurance company from New York had just called the office to see if the Undercover Brother was available to help them look into a robbery claim. One of their insured customers filed a claim against some expensive jewelry they asserted went missing during a break-in at their house.

The company's in-house investigator who worked in the Midwest territory passed away unexpectedly and they needed to hire someone fast. The insured client was pestering them for a payout. They were in a bind.

The money they offered initially was my daily per diem plus expenses. I knew the offer should be higher. My previous employer Ralph Dowden always got paid a percentage of the value of any recovered losses. I passed that information to Thelma. She sensed the company would pay more, so she negotiated on my behalf. When she balked at the original offer of per diem, the company's representative sweetened it to include 10% of any amount the agency recaptured from the theft. That meant this case could become mine and Thelma's biggest payday ever.

We agreed to a contract and the insurance company, UltaESurety, assigned a local administrator to work with me to track my progress and answer questions I might have during the investigation. Thelma arranged a videoconference with their administrator, Kalee Murphy, to discuss the process, the company's expectations, and to arrange reimbursements. I put the dog poisoning job on hold and headed to the office to join Thelma and Kalee on the video call.

Based on the screenshot, Ms. Murphy appeared to be an attractive young woman. With dark hair, fair skin, and a bright smile, I estimated her to be about twenty-five or thirty years old. Her age belied her strict business persona. She was serious about her work. A rare commodity these days.

Likewise, I think it startled her when she saw my image, a thirty-year-old man, pop up on her video screen. Most of the Private Investigators she had worked with were crusty old ex-cops or former military bad guys who used brute force methods to intimidate suspects. Kalee and I shared the bond of being blossoming young professionals.

Sticking to our assigned scripts, that first video chat went quickly. But I knew we would be in regular communication as the case progressed. By the third time we spoke, a friendship was already forming. It was business, but I had already decided that if this investigation went well, I would invite Kalee out for a celebratory drink to cement our new friendship.

The insured customers, Juris and Elsea Scratem, a husband-and-wife team, operated a cleaning business that serviced both corporate and residential customers. Successful immigrants from Eastern Europe, their business had grown to include eight employees comprising three cleaning crews. From outward appearances, they appeared to be your classic American dream story.

Kalee forwarded Thelma digital copies of the client's claim, a copy of the police report they filed, and the pertinent sections of their policy that applied to their claim. She also sent full descriptions of the jewelry. The email Kalee sent to us in the transmission included pictures of the larger pieces. The list included a diamond and ruby-studded necklace set in platinum and a matching set of earrings that appeared too large and heavy to be worn any length of time. There were three rings listed, one with multiple diamonds and the other two having multi-carat emerald stones. All in all, the claim listed fourteen items of various styles and values. She had copies of the original ten-year-old appraisals for the larger pieces, which amounted to over one hundred twenty thousand dollars. The client claimed that the current market value had risen to two hundred forty-five thousand dollars. More than double their original purchase price.

The policy had a maximum payout of over one million, so the client probably thought their two hundred forty-five thousand-dollar claim was a sure thing. They assumed the company would just cut a check and close the books. Kalee didn't say it directly, but she hinted that the company management suspected fraud.

I knew I had my work cut out for me. Doing a good job solving this case for them would lead to additional business. But how does one go about finding jewelry that has gone missing? There were no simple answers. The owner might simply be hiding the jewels in their mattress and claim someone stole them. If they were hiding the jewels somewhere, we would need to involve the police to obtain a search warrant. Or they could claim they were stolen, hock them at a pawn shop for whatever they could get, and then receive the insurance company's settlement. A double payout.

I had to assume the second scenario. My thinking was, if they were desperate for money, why hide the jewels?

I spent the first few days perusing the high-end Jewelry and Loan companies in the rich western suburbs. Unlike the grungy pawn shops in downtown Chicago, these places avoided the word "pawn" in their business name.

Instead, they pretended to be exclusive lenders to those wealthy clients with temporary cash flow problems. Their stores typically were clean and bright, looking more like a high-end retailer than a discount seller. The well-dressed employees wore business suits and had nicely manicured hands. Most had private offices where the client could discuss their financial situation with the appraiser in confidence.

Still, a pawn shop is a pawn shop. The only difference between the high-end stores in the suburbs and the low-end pawn shops in the city is the rich stores had greater financial resources to take on high-end merchandise.

It was a shot in the dark, finding the missing jewels on the market so soon after their disappearance. Still, it was worth the effort. People in a hurry make mistakes.

At the inner-city pawn shops, gathering information on where a product came from was easy. For a ten-dollar bill folded neatly in half and slipped into a friendly handshake, the guy behind the counter becomes very verbose. In five minutes, you walk away with some "I know a guy, who knows a guy" type of information.

It was different in the high-end suburban stores. Slipping a salesclerk ten dollars won't get you anything but a chuckle. I needed to take a different approach. Most pawn shops are legitimate businesses that want to project their image as reliable good guys.

I started by making a few trips to well-known loan companies and asking a few questions, but my initial search yielded no results. When I concluded that it wasn't going to be simple to recover the missing goods, I upped my level of intensity. Any legitimate store keeps excellent records and is in constant communication with local law enforcement.

Because they want to keep their reputation clean, the best way to gather information from them is through intimidation. If the proprietor thinks the law is after them, they sing like a nightingale on a summer's evening. I made it known the insurance company was serious and if we caught them buying stolen goods, they would have the cops on them so fast their heads would spin.

After checking out a few high-end loan companies in the western suburbs, I second-guessed my approach to finding the jewels. I was just about to give up when I wandered into a shop called Synergy Asset Lenders in Hinsdale, IL. Synergy Asset Lenders, in business for many years, had a stellar reputation for helping rich businesspeople attain short-term financing. High-end merchandise was their specialty.

Synergy Asset Lenders occupied space in a large mall with notable retail shops where Hinsdale's population of wealthy, old-money residents shopped for specialty goods. The retail showroom was well-lit, clean, and organized. A long glass counter housed expensive jewelry and precious antiques. Near the back, they displayed larger items, like furniture, paintings, and sculptures. The presence of security cameras monitoring the sales floor was obvious.

When I entered the door, an attractive young woman in a gray pantsuit extended her hand as she approached. She probably thought I was there to buy some jewelry as a gift for my wife or girlfriend. When I introduced myself and requested her help to complete my mission, her enthusiasm disappeared. She wanted to make a sale. If I wasn't buying, she would have no interest in helping me. But when I pointed out the seriousness of my cause, she pointed toward an elderly man seated in a private cubicle near the back. She said, "You're going to need to speak with Sy. He's the boss."

Sy Setzer was a short, balding man, about 5 feet 2 inches tall with an ample belly and buttocks to match.

I introduced myself and stressed the importance of my business.

Sy was surprisingly forthcoming. "A lady came in here two days ago with some high-end stuff. A necklace and a set of matching earrings. She wanted to know what I would give her. I suspected she was in distress, so I lowballed her. She didn't seem ready to negotiate. I knew what it was worth, but I wasn't sure if she was serious. We talked a little longer. She hinted there was more where this came from."

"What did she look like?"

"Blonde, well-dressed, attractive. She had a big rock on her left finger. Looked like a wedding ring. Usually, when it is an estate sale, the husband comes in to talk with us. Since she came alone, I figured maybe she was getting ready to leave her husband. That happens a lot. They sell their stuff before the lawyers get their hands on it."

I showed Sy a picture of one of the necklaces. "Was it like this one?"

"To be honest, I don't remember. She didn't seem to want to negotiate. Maybe she got scared. She just took her stuff and walked out. I figured she would be back."

Investigations start with fragments of information until someone slips up and reveals more than they should.

I surmised that if she went to one broker, she may have tried another. I reprised my intimidation act at a second loan company called Second Time Around, a couple of miles down the road.

This time, the guy at the store who called himself Thomas, was more knowledgeable and outgoing.

"She said her name was Elsea. She seemed a bit apprehensive. Said the jewelry was from her mother's estate. I didn't question her, but it didn't look old enough to be estate jewelry. The hallmark suggested it was made within the past decade. It isn't the type of stuff you see in estate sales. I made her an excellent offer, but she didn't take it. I couldn't offer more. She stammered, then said she would be back with her husband."

I pointed toward the surveillance cameras in the corners of the room. "Any chance you might have her picture on video?"

Glancing up toward a camera near the rear of the offices, he said. "We might."

"How can I get a copy of the footage from that day?"

"Come back with a warrant, I suppose. We are very discreet here at Second Time."

I thanked Thomas for his help, suggesting he would hear from me again.

To me, it was obvious that the Scratems were trying to unload some of the jewelry they claimed someone stole from their house. Based on the information Kalee Murphy shared with me, we were on the right track.

After speaking again with Kalee via a video chat we agreed to offer a reward for information that leads to the recovery of the stolen goods. The reward idea worked, and I set up a sting operation with the proprietor at Second Time Around. Hopeful she would return with more of the treasure trove, I asked him to contact me immediately if the lady named Elsea should return with her husband. I thought they might make a final push to unload the merchandise before they got caught. Thinking we were on the right track, I waited, hoping something would pop and she would return to Second Time Around. A few days went by, but the Scratem's and merchandise didn't show up.

I was making progress, albeit slowly. Trying to keep the momentum going, I cast the net a little wider by badgering the counter guys at a few of the sketchy pawn shops in the inner city. Dealing with these guys differs from the suburban shops. The inner-city guys are tougher and have more experience with petty thieves. While they are more tuned into and aware of stolen goods, they also know how to fence hot merchandise without getting their fingers burned.

I started at Southside Lending, which turned out to be more of a resale shop than a broker. Much of their inventory was furniture and musical instruments. I didn't see the type of high-end jewelry the Scratem's reported stolen. The saleswoman at Southside shook her head when I asked about diamonds and gems.

Next, I visited ABC Pawn, a rundown storefront in the sleazy part of town. The people I encountered there intimidated me, but I kept my head high and acted authoritatively.

The crusty inner-city guys are pretty tight-lipped when talking about who is selling stolen goods. They deal with undercover cops more often. The counter clerk at ABC Pawn couldn't remember hearing about any hot merchandise, but after slipping him a twenty-dollar bill, his memory got better.

He folded the twenty into his shirt pocket and tapped his finger to his head as if he were trying to recall. "You know, I think I heard something about some primo stuff coming available. Some necklaces and earrings. Diamonds, stuff like that," he said.

"Where can I get some of that primo stuff?" I asked.

"You didn't hear it from me, but I heard one of the local loan sharks bought an expensive necklace for his girlfriend. A guy named Benny."

"Where can I find Benny?" I asked.

"He owns a nightclub out by the airport. I don't remember the name of the club, but just ask around. Everyone knows Big Benny."

One phone call to Thelma and ten minutes of research yielded the name Ben "Big Benny" Archane. Big Benny, the owner of a topless dance club, had a reputation for helping people solve their cash flow problems at higher-than-average interest rates. Benny dealt in cash, most of it in small bills like fives and tens. A trip to Benny's club, to scope out the scene, was in order.

I had a challenge on my hands. The clerk at ABC Pawn hinted that Benny was a tough cookie. No one to be trifled with. I had no desire to make a return trip to the forest preserve, to be beaten and bloodied.

The next night, I strapped my Baretta into its holster under my arm, pulled on a one-size-too-large sports jacket, and headed north toward the airport. Forty minutes later, I was walking into The Kandy Shop, a late-night gentlemen's club.

Despite its name on the sign out front, gentlemen seldom frequented The Kandy Shop. Most of the patrons I saw were creepy old men or rough-looking thugs who looked like they could snap your neck with their bare hands and enjoy doing it. Like a lion tamer who enters the cage with just a whip and a chair, I had to keep my eyes on everyone at once.

I quickly scanned the room to assess its layout. Toward the back of the room sat a U-shaped stage. The stage was ringed with tables and chairs strategically placed, so each seat gave the patrons a close-up view of the dancers.

To the right of the entranceway, near the emergency exit, his back to the wall, sat a huge black man, whom I targeted to be Big Benny. Flanking Benny were two muscular gang bangers, one on each side. They formed a de facto shield around their boss. Both men vigilantly scanned the room to ensure everyone in the bar maintained their proper behavior.

The girls at The Kandy Shop were pretty and friendly. My immediate assessment said most of them looked too young to be strippers and certainly below the legal drinking age. They were probably runaways from a small town, or desperate girls trafficked in from Central American countries.

Despite being a single man in his late twenties, this wasn't my scene. I despised characters like Big Benny, who took advantage of innocent young girls. Benny, a small-time criminal, had a lengthy rap sheet, but somehow operated within the fringes of the legal system. I was no angel, but compared to Benny, I looked like a saint.

Not wanting to attract attention, I sat down at a table one row back, away from the stage. I could see a direct pathway to the door marked the emergency exit. I wasn't sure where that doorway led, but I hoped it was a path to safety should something go wrong, and I needed a quick exit. Assuming I could get past Benny and his henchmen.

My next move was to figure out some way to engage Benny in conversation. My goal was to make them think I wanted to buy expensive jewelry at a discount. If I could get Benny's attention without raising a red flag, I might get a lead on the stolen goods.

Rather than approach Big Benny directly, I tried a more subtle approach. The young woman who was servicing the tables, although half naked, decked herself out in loads of costume jewelry. I engaged her in conversation, complimenting her on her style and asking where she got her earrings and rings. After examining her bangles closely, I suggested I might like something a little higher quality.

"I want something expensive. Where can I get a high-class necklace and some diamond earrings? I have cash."

She hinted she might know a guy. That was all she said.

I sat sipping my beer and watched the pretty young dancers parade around on and off the stage. My frustration was growing as nearly an hour went by and I failed to get Benny's attention.

Just as I was considering a different approach, the young woman returned to my table. She showed me a ring she wasn't wearing earlier. It seemed better in quality compared to the costume jewelry she wore initially.

I hinted that my need was for a love interest. "I'm not really after a ring today. We are going to a party. I need a necklace and earrings." Winking at her, I said, "If she likes the necklace and earrings, I might come back for the ring."

She smiled at me, then looking back at Benny seated across the room, she pointed toward me. He nodded, and she said, "Maybe Benny can help you. Why don't you follow me?"

I followed her to Benny's table, where he motioned for me to sit. The two big goons flanking Benny made a point of moving their chairs into a defensive position so that if I tried anything risky, they would stop me.

"I understand you are in the market for some high-end bling?"

"Yes, something with diamonds. A necklace or earrings, or both."

Benny slid a box covered with burgundy felt across the table. I opened the box. Inside was a necklace. It looked the same as the picture that Kalee Murphy sent to Thelma.

"I have the matching earrings in the safe," he said.

"How much?" I asked.

"Twenty-five for the necklace and five for the earrings."

Pretending to be flummoxed by the price, I said. "I didn't bring that much cash. I'm gonna need about one hour. Hold them for me? I will be back."

I slid the box back across the table. Benny stared at me. His look worried me. I thought I had played a bad hand. Then his two bodyguards slid back in their chairs, leaving me an escape route.

"I am here all night," he said. "The goods might be here later, or maybe they'll be gone. There are a lot of people looking for quality stuff."

"I'll be back in an hour," I repeated.

There was no doubt in my mind the jewelry Benny was peddling was Juris and Elsea Scratem's. Whether he stole them in a robbery or was fencing them for the Scratems wasn't my concern. I had to work fast. I called Kalee Murphy to report my progress. It was after normal business hours, but I could not wait. I told her about my encounter with Benny Archane and how I was sure he was fencing the Scratem's jewelry. Kalee's voice filled with excitement. She wanted to move quickly.

Kalee had the direct number of a detective who worked in the Illinois State Police Crime Suppression Unit. The detective, Ari Treski, had been tracking "Big Benny" Archane for months. Until today, Treski could never catch him red-handed. He was salivating at the chance of putting Benny out of business.

It all happened unexpectedly fast. In less than an hour, I met Treski in the parking lot next to The Kandy Shop. He handed me an envelope and told me to go inside and pretend to purchase the necklace. He said he would follow me in. Little did I know, two of Treski's deputies were already inside, waiting for me to make the deal.

When I told Big Benny I would be back in an hour, he didn't expect me to come back with a team of law enforcement officers. I cautiously approached Benny, his henchmen, watching my every move. I slid the envelope across the table and Benny slid the necklace and earrings to me.

Before I could even react, Treski and his men announced themselves as police, confiscating both the jewelry and the payment envelope. Seconds later, Benny Archane was in handcuffs, and I was scurrying out the door under the protection of the Illinois State Police.

Treski and his team recovered ten pieces of jewelry, including a diamond ring, an emerald bracelet, and three strings of pearls from Scratem's collection. The value totaled one hundred fifty thousand dollars, of which my agency is due ten percent as my reward for recovery.

As expected, Big Benny threw Juris Scratem under the bus, copping a plea. He claimed he didn't know the merchandise was stolen. Benny claimed he purchased the jewelry fair and square for cash from a needy owner. Despite his plea, Treski charged Big Benny with Receiving Stolen Property, a felony.

Kaylee Murphy was ecstatic that we could recover the missing pieces. Even though she was just a local administrator, it reflected well on her career by managing a high-value recovery. Based on the outcome of any legal action, her company would deny Scratem's claims, saving them substantial money.

It would be my largest invoice to date and my success with Scratem's case virtually guaranteed I would get more business from UltaESurety. Even better, other specialty insurance companies would take note of the recovery. As the word spreads, more commissions will result.

Heartened by my success, I sat at my desk, wondering what I should do with the money. "Do I take a vacation, or should I start a retirement account?" I thought.

It was the most money I earned since I shook hands with Valter Zermenski and started my agency. Still, after setting aside money for this month's rent and paying off my credit card debt, there wasn't enough to retire on. Instead, I shared my payout with my Undercover Sister, Thelma Jenkins. I knew she needed the money more than me. The rest I put in the bank for a rainy-day fund.

While the investigation was brief, Kalee and I had become friends. Several times during our conversations, I was positive she was flirting with me. So, as promised, I invited Kalee out for a celebratory drink. We met at a trendy bar in Chicago's River North neighborhood. I really liked Kalee's look. I thought we might make an attractive couple. A smart and friendly young woman, she made it perfectly clear she wasn't looking to establish a romantic relationship with me or any man. She had a girlfriend at home who met all her needs.

It turns out I was probably wrong about the flirting. We weren't each other's type. We are still friends and colleagues, nevertheless.

THE BERWYN BENEFIT

My return to life back in Berwyn had its benefits. It reconnected me with my family and old friends from the neighborhood. My parents live only about ten minutes from my office, so I try to check up on them as often as possible. When my dad retired, he took up the hobby of trying to invent a better mousetrap. Being a Mechanical Engineer, he was good with tools and building things. He liked to putter around in the garage on his latest project.

Because of his age, it worried my mom when Dad took on bigger projects than he was capable of completing. He might injure himself or blow up the garage or cause some other accident. To be sure he was safe and sound, she called me to come to their house to check on him. Most of the time, Leon was fine. He had been a brilliant engineer for thirty years. His aptitude for mechanical things was unchallenged. He was smarter than me, so there was little risk of harm. Occasionally, he would start a project that was beyond the physical ability of a sixty-five-year-old man. That's when I stepped in to supply some additional muscle or help him with a computer program.

Checking up on Dad helped me as well. It gave us a chance to bond again. We weren't just father and son; we became friends, equals, two men who enjoyed each other's company.

A couple of days before Thanksgiving, my mom called to ask for help. I used the excuse of helping with the Thanksgiving holiday dinner to stop by and visit the garage. I used that time to see what I could do to help my dad with his latest endeavor.

My dad had gotten himself involved in a project that included rebuilding the motor from an old classic Rambler automobile. Parts for the old car were scarce, so he was machining his own replacements. My job was to crawl under the car to take measurements or make a trial fitment of the part, something I could do more easily than he could.

We were working on fitting a newly designed alternator mounting bracket for the Rambler when we noticed a car cruising past our house at a ridiculously slow pace. The car made several passes, pausing suspiciously, then driving on down the street. After it drove past our house, the car would disappear around the corner, only to return and drive by again minutes later.

At first, we passed it off as someone being lost. But being suspicious, I noted the make and model of the car. The car was a white, late-model Mercedes-Benz convertible. This wasn't a run-of-the-mill C-series Benz. It was a high-end SL63 model with the letters AMG proudly displayed on the rear deck. That model sported a price tag that likely exceeded two hundred thousand dollars. Expensive cars like that are sorely out of place in Berwyn's lower-middle-class neighborhood, where the neighbors considered my Dad's two-year-old Buick opulent.

It was unlikely the driver of that car was a burglar casing the neighborhood. The person who drove that expensive car was rich. The car alone costs as much as the houses in this part of town. If they were cat burglars, looking for an easy score, they were in the wrong place.

I climbed out from under Dad's Rambler and waited as the car made another pass. When it approached again, I stepped outside our garage. I ran toward the street, to get a better look before the car disappeared. The driver's face wasn't visible, but I made a mental note of the color and model. Just before they sped away, I caught a partial glimpse of the license plate. I could tell it wasn't an Illinois plate, but I didn't get the numbers. If I had gotten the numbers, it would be easy to figure out who was behind this suspicious behavior.

After I left my parents' house, I detoured on my way home, spending a few minutes cruising around my old neighborhood. I hoped to catch a glimpse of the suspicious Mercedes-Benz parked at one of the neighbors' houses. As I patrolled the neighborhood, I cruised past my old girlfriend Jessica's house. Her parents, George and Marian Sekelsky, still lived in the same home where Jessica grew up. I had visited their home many times as a young man. I considered stopping to say hello, thinking it might be nice to see the Sekelskys again. Then I thought they might think I was spying on Jessica. Considering the way things ended between Jessica and me, it was probably best not to reopen old wounds.

All was quiet at Sekelsky's house. There was no sign of the high-end luxury car anywhere in the neighborhood. I chalked it up to happenstance, but I made a mental note to keep my eyes and ears open for unusual activities in the area.

IT CAN'T BE JESSICA SEKELSKY

It took me longer than I expected to find my niche in life. But after years of hard work, I am proud to say I am the most successful Private Investigator in Berwyn, Illinois. Accordingly, all of my business marketing materials, my business cards, and advertisements in the Yellow Pages proudly proclaim, "Berwyn's Number One Detective Agency". That distinction isn't as impressive as it sounds, because mine is the only private investigator agency in Berwyn, Illinois. Still, that honor lets me lay claim to the award of being the best. Everyone wants to be the best, no matter what they do. I am no different.

My business was growing. It wasn't long before I developed a reputation for unearthing even the deepest, darkest secrets someone might be hiding. If someone was covering up a legal or immoral action, Able Body was the guy who could piece together the puzzle. And, depending on how busy I was, I could also help locate a missing uncle or find a lost puppy if someone needed help with those things.

Things were going well. I even had my emergency fund in the bank in case business slowed. Then, one afternoon, as I prepared myself for an evening of surveillance of a possibly wayward spouse, storm clouds formed on the horizon.

I was eating a late lunch at one of the fast-food restaurants that ringed the courtyard of the Oakbrook Center shopping mall. The town of Oakbrook, Illinois, just west of Berwyn, is a more upscale suburb than my hometown. It's home to rich business executives, renowned doctors, and prominent lawyers who had their professional offices in the big city and hosted their cocktail parties in the suburbs. The Oakbrook Center mall is the place where their wives and trendy suburban influencers gather to see and be seen.

I was seated near a window watching the older socialite women with their Gucci bags and the younger soccer moms in their tight leggings saunter past. Both were at the mall to spend their rich husband's money. As they strolled by me, dangling from their arms were shopping bags filled with designer clothes, jewelry, and perfumes. It was then I noticed something unexpected. Seated on a bench outside in the courtyard area was a fair-skinned, dark-haired woman, dressed in designer clothes. I would not have thought much about her presence except that she had a remarkable resemblance to someone I knew from the past, Jessica Belle Sekelsky. The woman appeared to be watching me through the window. It was a crazy feeling because I was the one whose job it was to watch other people. I seldom had people watching me.

Unnerved, I quickly chomped down the last of my sandwich and slurped the last of my soft drink. The rattling sound from the straw sucking the bottom of my cup brought the young woman who serviced the tables over to me. Politely she asked, "Would you like a refill, Sir?"

Her question distracted me enough to take my eyes off the woman seated outside.

"No," I said.

I handed her the tray with the used wrappers and empty cup and bolted out the door to confront my observer. Except, by the time I got to where she was seated, she was gone. I scanned the crowded walkway area of the mall, hoping to catch a glimpse of her walking away. All I could see were busy men and women shoppers browsing the storefronts, pointing at displays, and then moving on down the mall. In a matter of seconds, the woman who looked like Jessica disappeared, nowhere to be found.

I looked at my watch, making note of the time. Ralph Dowden taught me to always note the time of any event no matter how inconsequential it may seem.

There wasn't time to investigate further. I had a job a few miles down the road and I needed to begin my next assignment. Starting today, I promised a new client I would stake out a business in the nearby suburb of Downers Grove. It seems a young doctor was putting in extra hours at the office and his wife was nervous. She wasn't sure if she should be concerned about his patient load and how hard he was working, or worried about his relationship with his receptionist. She hired me to figure out which of these two activities the doctor needed to curtail.

I found my car in the mall parking garage and headed west to the address of the doctor's office, where I camped out doing what I do best, watching and waiting.

From across the parking lot, where he ran his practice, I watched the doctor's patients come and go. I observed the doctor appeared to be keeping longer than advertised hours at his office. One concern the doctor's wife, my client, had expressed to me was the relationship between the doctor and his receptionist. Was he putting in overtime of a romantic nature?

I took note that the receptionist left the office a few minutes past 5:30 p.m., while additional patients came and went until nearly 8:00 p.m. It seemed the doctor either preferred working over being home with his wife, or he needed to make more money to keep her happily well off. "Unhappy at home or simply an enthusiastic good guy?" I wondered, which was it?

I repeated my surveillance of Doctor Good Guy one more day, taking a few pictures and making notes for my report. He repeated the same sequence, his receptionist leaving work on time and him working additional hours until late in the evening, alone. To me, it was obvious. Doctor Good Guy wasn't cheating on his wife, just working overtime to make extra money.

I watched Doctor Good Guy working late into the evening. I had no way of knowing how much money the doctor was making working late, but some of the money he made working overtime his wife was using to pay my fees. Sort of ironic.

While I sat watching and waiting, my mind returned to Jessica. The woman I saw at the mall appeared older, more serious looking than I remembered, but every bit as beautiful. There was no question it was Jessica I saw at the mall.

I asked myself. "What was she doing there? Why did she disappear so quickly?"

Her sudden reappearance had me wondering why she was following me when she could call or come to my office. Jessica was always a bit of a drama queen. It would be a few more days before I found out.

Because I work late-night hours, I often sleep late in the morning and don't show up at the office until the afternoon. Thelma does a good job of arranging my client appointments to fit my schedule. Usually, in the afternoon.

Last Friday, I walked into the office late, around 5:25 p.m. Thelma was already packing up her belongings for the day.

"How'd everything go today, Thelma?" I asked.

"It was quiet. I have been trying to get that priest to leave a retainer. He is still hedging. Says he wants to talk with you again. I don't think he is on board, at least with the fee you quoted him. He is praying you will work pro bono."

The priest she was talking about believed one of his altar boys was being abused at home. He didn't want to call the police without evidence. He asked me to snoop around to see what I could discover. While I felt sorry for the boy, it was a matter for the police and social services to investigate. Besides, the priest had no money. He instead offered me a place in heaven as my reward for helping him. While I am not against religion and would love a reservation in heaven in my name, I was skeptical about his ability to guarantee me a spot in an everlasting paradise.

"Oh," Thelma said. "That woman called three times today. She asked to speak to you. As soon as I say you are out of the office, she hangs up. She has the Caller ID blocked on her phone, so I can't see the number she's calling from. No message and I can't call her back. You really should look into this. Perhaps I should give her your cell phone number so she can call you directly?"

The idea of giving out my private number to a non-paying customer did not appeal to me. I found that giving out my cell phone number, even to paying customers, was a big mistake. People call at inappropriate times, for the silliest reasons. At least I can bill paying customers.

"No," I replied. "Let's see if you can convince her to leave her number."

Private Investigators get a lot of crank calls. Most are inquiries from suspicious people unsure if they want to start an investigation. They are confused and don't know who else to call. When they find out their suspicions could amount to hundreds or thousands of dollars worth of effort and expense, they hang up and never call back. Most of my paying clients are like the wife of Doctor Good Guy, who spent several hundred dollars learning that her husband worked overtime to make extra money so he could buy her nice things. All she had to do was ask him why he was working so late.

I get calls from people who are writing mystery novels. They fall in love with the mystique of the steamy detective novel and think a Private Investigator will give them insight into a unique storyline they can write about. After speaking with me, they realize my investigations are mostly boring and costly. Using my experiences as a plot will probably result in a book that will never get published or read by anyone.

Seeing Jessica, or the woman who reminded me of Jessica, stirred up the feelings that I had been suppressing for years. When I returned to Berwyn, I forced myself to forget Jessica and the days of our youth. There was no sense pining over what might have been. Her possible reappearance made me want to know more. So, at the risk of reopening my old wounds, I asked Thelma to research the names Barry and Jessica McGleam of Massachusetts. I wanted to learn as much as possible about how Barry and Jessica's lives had developed since she and I went our separate ways almost ten years ago.

Thelma was like a pit bull, pulling together a dossier that painted a revealing picture of the lives of two of Boston's elite citizens. I soon learned that Barry became a successful corporate lawyer, one of the more lucrative legal specialties in the county of Norfolk, MA, an area of old money. His family's connections to investment bankers, business executives, and corporate moguls greased the skids for his law firm to succeed.

Barry made millions of dollars defending big corporations against lawsuits from plaintiffs that charged them with every form of incompetence or wrongdoing. Despite advertising himself as a trial lawyer, he seldom went to trial. Most often, he would negotiate a settlement for the defendant that included no admission of guilt.

Reading about Barry's business model made me smile. I remembered the sign I used to see on Ralph Dowden's office wall. "We all deserve justice. Most people can't afford it." Time and time again, Barry McGleam's law firm proved money can buy justice.

Barry's success in defending the wealthy made him a known quantity. His big name and substantial bank accounts earned him membership into the inner circle in Norfolk County who's who. After a few years, Barry became bored with corporate law and became involved in politics. With the help of a hired political consultant, Barry aligned himself with the soon-to-be retiring District Attorney, Tommy Boyle.

Barry handed his lucrative corporate clients over to the junior partners at his law firm. That is when Barry began working alongside Boyle's office in a crusade to prosecute the organized crime operations that were growing more sophisticated and wealthier. Boyle wanted to retire and leave public office with the legacy that he "cleaned up the town", and Barry wanted to help him.

With Boyle's blessing, Barry was the favorite to replace him as the voter's choice in the upcoming general election. Barry's well-funded campaign and unsullied track record skyrocketed him into the forefront of Massachusetts politics.

With only weeks before the election, the polls showed Barry had a substantial lead over Boyle's long-time rival and conservative opponent, Wallace Bolton. Bolton, who claimed to be a law-and-order candidate, constantly attacked Barry's squeaky clean image. Nothing ever stuck. The more mud Bolton threw at him, the better Barry looked. Barry's campaign manager portrayed him as a man just one step shy of canonization.

Bolton had the opposite problem. He frequently found his name associated with organized crime. Despite his desperate attempts to clean up his image, he couldn't distance himself from that perception. Barry's campaign staff exploited Bolton's shortcomings whenever it could. They even accused Bolton of being involved in the mysterious and unsolved death of his brother some twenty years earlier.

Barring any unforeseen developments, Barry McGleam was a shoo-in to be the next Norfolk County District Attorney.

When I read about Barry's success, it chaffed at my bottom. Barry had everything a man could want. He had money, a successful career, and the respect of his peers, and of course, I never forgot he had stolen Jessica. From outward appearances, Jessica had achieved the stature she so desperately craved. Barry's money and influence positioned her as an elite socialite in Norfolk County. Jessica, although no longer a practicing attorney, maintained her membership in the Massachusetts Bar Association, where she continued to serve as an ambassador, a mostly ceremonial position. She could have been a successful trial lawyer in her own right but accepted the role of Barry's wife to help promote his career over hers.

Because of her involvement in helping Barry with his campaign for District Attorney, Jessica was often the target of Wallace Bolton's campaign staff. They went out of their way to paint her as disingenuous, dishonest, and in some cases, coquettish.

The woman I saw at Oakbrook Mall had to be Jessica. If true, there were many questions to be asked and answered.

"Why was she in Chicago and not in Boston with her husband?" "Is she the woman who keeps calling my office without leaving a message or contact information?" "Could she be the driver of the car that drove past my parents' house?" "Was she trying to contact me because she was in trouble?"

All these questions made me want to know more. The problem was, to me, Jessica was poison. No, correct that. Poison is not the right word. She was more like an addiction. Poison kills. Addictions may not kill you, but they stay with you your whole life. She had ruined my life once. If not for Jessica, I would today be a successful, albeit unhappy, mechanical engineer.

Like everyone else in my family, I probably would have settled for an average-looking girl, bought an average house, and had average-looking children of average intelligence. I could have just followed in my parents' footsteps, working a nine-to-five job just to pay my bills, until I got old and retired.

Instead, my life is now a series of late-night stakeouts, drinking whiskey from a bottle hidden in my desk drawer, and fantasizing over an affair with an overweight black woman fifteen years my elder.

Despite not wishing to reopen my past with Jessica, since her reappearance, I could not get her out of my mind. I intended to get to the bottom of this untimely interruption.

Being in politics, Barry McGleam's life, at least his professional life, became something of an open book. That meant I could easily dig into Barry's present profile, and maybe even into his sordid past.

Mounted on the wall in my office was a large whiteboard. I used it as a mind map to piece together clues whenever an investigation took on greater depth than I could keep organized with paper and pen. It was both magnetic and worked with dry-erase markers, allowing me to post documents, pictures, and newspaper clippings, and then use a marker to make notes of their relevancy.

I started building a profile of the life Barry and Jessica had created. To me, it all seemed too perfect. No one's life is that good. Too perfect leads to questions. Everyone has skeletons in their closets. "What was the skeleton in their closet?" I thought.

Then, a few days ago, the answers to several of my questions arrived.

I was taking a nap on the couch in my office. I had been on a stakeout all night and could barely keep my eyes open. Thelma in the outer office answered my phone calls and made sure I was undisturbed. Around 5:30 p.m., Thelma shut down the office and was preparing to leave when the phone rang. She answered it quickly, but the noise awoke me from a sound sleep. A few seconds later, she peeked into my office to check on me. Seeing me stirring, she said, "It was that woman again. No Caller ID, no message. She just asked for Mr. Bōdyē. When I said you were unavailable, she hung up. Maybe she will call back. I can stay a little longer if you need me."

"That's okay Thelma," I replied. You should go home. Your family needs you more than me."

I got up from the couch and went to the bathroom. After splashing some water on my face and brushing my teeth, I felt better. By the time I emerged from the toilet, Thelma had already gone home, and I was alone again. That's when a realization came to me. Thelma said, "She just asked for Mr. Bōdyē." The caller used the correct pronunciation of my name. Only people who already knew me intimately called me Mr. Bōdyē. Regular people or potential clients call me Able Body.

With nowhere else to go, I sat down at my desk to ponder what the hell was going on. Reaching into my desk drawer, I poured myself an ounce of my favorite Irish Whiskey. While I waited for my laptop to boot up and connect to the Wi-Fi, I stared at the whiteboard with the preliminary information I had collected on Barry and Jessica. I contemplated what I might do if I found something of interest in either of their profiles. I questioned myself,

"Would I reveal it to the world? Could I use this information to gain revenge on Barry?"

Then reality crept back into my head. "Why should I care?" I thought. Even more so, I wondered, "Why should I get involved?"

At precisely 6:41 p.m., many of the questions spinning around in my head were answered.

As I stared at the whiteboard, I heard a soft voice coming from the outer office. When Thelma left at 5:30 p.m., I was still in the bathroom. Knowing I was still working, or at least still at my desk, she probably didn't bother to lock the front door of the offices. She assumed I would lock up when I left for the day. During that time, anyone could come in. It sounded as if someone did.

Before I could respond, the voice called out again, "Hello, is anyone here?"

I jumped from my seat and opened the inner office door and peered into the reception area. There she was, the woman of my dreams, Jessica Belle Sekelsky-McGleam. She was several years older than I remembered, but every bit as beautiful.

One glance made me remember why I fell for her. Her dark hair now longer, added a sultry characteristic to her once innocent image. Her face was fuller and her once slender figure more shapely, like an hourglass.

She looked straight at me without saying a word. I froze in my tracks, not sure how I should react. "Do I smile and say hello? Should I tell her to go away, leave me in peace, and slam the door?" I thought.

Still stunned by her presence. I couldn't think of anything brilliant, so I said, "Jessica, what are you doing here?"

"Hi Able, you look well."

Stymied for something more to say, I repeated, "What are you doing here?"

"Oh, Able. I am so sorry about what happened to us. If you never speak to me again, I'll understand. I'm scared and didn't know where else to turn."

A flood of emotions coursed through my body. At first, it was anger. "How could she?" I thought. I remembered how abandoned I felt, how I had given up my plans and my future to stay with her in Massachusetts, only to have her choose Barry McGleam instead of me. Then a ray of hope slipped through. She was my first love. I thought, "Was she coming back?"

As I felt myself softening. I took one last stab at resistance.

"Why aren't you with Barry? Why are you here?"

"My marriage is falling apart. Barry is cheating on me. He has a mistress. I have known for some time. Able, I am a kept woman. I want out of this marriage, but I need proof of his infidelity. I can't let him get away with his lying anymore."

A smart man would have told her to leave. I would have shut the door and returned to my mediocre life as the number one private investigator in Berwyn. Instead, I motioned for her to come inside. "Sit down, talk to me. I need to know more."

Jessica stepped further into the office and looked around. She frowned, half in revulsion, half in pity at the way I lived. She had grown accustomed to a luxurious lifestyle. Looking at my dimly lit office full of old, used furniture and rumpled leather couch told her she was wise to choose Barry over me. Her eyes flicked toward the bottle of cheap whisky and half-filled glass parked atop the desk. She said nothing.

"When did you get back?" I asked.

"About a week ago. Barry and I had a big fight. I threatened to expose his infidelities. His election for District Attorney is in a couple of weeks. A scandal would jeopardize his election. He said if I leaked his affair before the election, I would regret it. After the election, he would talk about a divorce settlement. We have a pretty comprehensive pre-nuptial agreement, so the issue isn't money. But I still don't trust him."

"Do you think he would hurt you?" I asked.

"I don't know. Barry's always been a paper tiger. He owes a lot of people favors. There's no telling what kind of pressure he is under. But his threatening tone scared me. I had to get away from him."

"What do you expect me to do? You're a lawyer, drag him into court."

Then her face changed. Instantly, she became that persuasive young girl who could make me do anything she asked. It felt like we had returned to high school.

"Save me. Help me. Able, I need to start again. I want to make up for my past mistakes."

This time, I wasn't about to take the bait. I stood my ground. "Jessica, you need a lawyer, not a lover. Sorry, I am not for sale."

My initial resistance meant it was time for Jessica's next act. The tears streamed down her face. "Oh Able, I have made a mess of my life. I guess I just needed someone friendly to talk with."

"Jessica," I said. "Go home, confront Barry, and get your life back in order. Then, when you have settled your problems, we can talk."

Bravery doesn't normally extend to personal relationships, yet it was the bravest thing I've ever done. Jessica had always been my kryptonite. This time, I wouldn't let her manipulate me. I wheeled around to the front of my desk. "Give me a minute."

I opened the screen of my laptop and began typing. In a few minutes, I had the names of lawyers in the Boston area I thought could help her. She probably already knew half of them, but I needed to pretend I was helping. I wrote several names on a slip of paper. My hands shook a little as I handed it to her.

She took the paper, then dipped her hand into her purse and pulled out a business card. "Here's my cellphone number if you change your mind."

She stood up, turned toward the door, and repeated her earlier plea. "Able, I am sorry. I promise I will make this right."

I watched her walk out the office door. I gave her time to make her way out of the building, then I checked the outer office. She was gone and, once again, I was alone. I locked the outer office door and went back to my desk. Jessica had left the building, but I knew she wasn't gone for good. My life was taking another U-turn.

IT'S NOT OVER UNTIL IT'S OVER

Like any good Private Detective, Able Body knows there is more to the story than meets the eye. Jessica's reappearance stirred something inside me, a curiosity I couldn't let go of without looking further. The words people use leave hints of deeper meaning. Some things she said invoked my interest. Jessica complained about Barry having a mistress. I always believed Jessica was a rare beauty. It made me wonder. "What woman had Barry found that is more desirable than Jessica?"

Being someone who cannot leave well enough alone, I knew with a little research, I could put an identity to Barry's female indiscretion.

I never considered myself to be a vindictive person, but if I knew the details of Barry's affair, I would have Barry by the balls. I hated Barry McGleam. If Jessica was afraid to blackmail Barry, I wasn't. I smiled, thinking after all these years in the battle between Able Body and Barry McGleam, I might have the upper hand. It brought to mind the old phrase, "Revenge is a dish best served cold."

The next morning, my phone dinged. It was a text from Jessica. "Thanks for your advice. I am heading back to Boston. This morning, I called one of those lawyers you gave me. I have a meeting scheduled with him on Wednesday. He says if I can show proof that Barry violated our prenuptial agreement, he is gonna be in deep shit."

I chose not to respond. Responding to her text might further implicate me in any plot Jessica was hatching. Instead, I continued my research into Barry's girlfriend. I had done this type of discovery before for divorce lawyers. If nothing else, any information I gathered might help Jessica in her divorce proceedings.

Internet research was a task I could do between other jobs, but since this was a personal matter, I prioritized it over less pressing issues. By digging down deep, I hoped to find as much negative shit about Barry as possible.

It didn't take me long to find out one of Barry's campaign staff workers was a young woman with a big mouth and breasts to match. The posts on her social media profile made her a loose cannon. They usually screen campaign workers and train them not to reveal private information about their candidates to the media and outsiders. This woman wasn't trained well.

Her social media profile showed pictures of parties and meetings with other dignitaries. Not always in the best light. She was leaving Barry susceptible to scandal.

Continuing with the profiles of some of Barry's other staff members, I stumbled across several articles posted last year that should have been marked for deletion, but someone overlooked them. The posts were complete with pictures of Barry enjoying himself on a business junket to Cabo San Lucas with a shapely young woman named Tiffany Burns. Tiffany had strawberry blonde hair, fair skin, and a bright smile. Her ample bosoms, round buttocks, and long legs gave her the star-like qualities you might see on a Hollywood big screen. In the photos, Tiffany wore a skimpy white string bikini that left little to the imagination.

The two seemed to be alone, and the pictures were racy. It was supposed to be a business trip, but the only business they appeared to be conducting was monkey business.

Surely, those pictures were information that Barry's opponent, Wallace Bolton, would love to have. It surprised me that no one from Bolton's campaign staff uncovered them and used them for his benefit. Perhaps Bolton also had skeletons in his closet he didn't want to be revealed. "Was there still honor among thieves?" I thought.

The woman, Tiffany Burns, intrigued me. It wasn't just her beauty, which was every bit equal to Jessica's. Because, even in a bikini, she had a classy style about her. I knew immediately I needed to look deeper into Tiffany's background. I wondered, "Who was she? Could she turn out to be Barry's Achilles' heel?"

It didn't take long to find a lot of information on Tiffany Burns. She worked as an exotic dancer at an upscale strip club named the Peppermint Lounge just outside Needham, MA. A little research identified the place as one that is frequented by wealthy business executives and dodgy politicians. The scuttlebutt on social media suggested that they passed more legislation on the barstools at the Peppermint Lounge than in the halls of government.

I wondered if Barry and Tiffany were more than just a romantic fling. Could Tiffany be working for Barry by acquiring insider information from unsuspecting clients and feeding it to Barry? Or could the reverse be true? Might Tiffany be gaining information from Barry to share with someone else?

The deeper I dug, the more the whole affair took on a soap opera sort of quality. The list of players that could wreak havoc on Barry's campaign and his political future surprised me. There was an entire cast and crew in plain view for anyone to see. "How had he remained so squeaky clean in the public eye?" I asked myself. "Why wasn't anyone paying attention?"

I have often wondered if, as a society, we have sunk so low into the mud that nothing shocks the voting public anymore. Inappropriate behavior is not only accepted, but also expected.

As usual, I found myself getting sucked into the drama. Like any good soap opera, you get pulled into watching and waiting for the next unlikely series of events to unfold before your eyes.

After assembling a considerable file on Tiffany Burns, I turned my sights to Wallace Bolton. Most politicians are pretty careful with posting on social media. They try to always portray a squeaky-clean image and only post more mundane topics, like wishing someone a happy birthday or buying a coffee at a local merchant. Images that cannot be twisted by opposing candidates. Bolton was no exception. He liked pictures of newborn babies, cute puppies, and little kittens. He was careful to only post pictures of flowers and sunsets on his social media feeds.

Still, social media can be a double-edged sword. Even if you're careful with your social media posts, your followers and friends may not be. Given enough time, perusing the feeds of someone's friends might reveal a hidden clue.

Bolton's social media friends list included a woman named Sarah Thomas. Sarah Thomas was far less cautious in attacking Barry McGleam and his candidacy for District Attorney than Bolton. She commented often on Barry's actions. It could just be the rancor from his past indiscretions, or it might unveil a more recent political motive. I knew that further research into Sarah's relationship with both Bolton and McGleam might yield some interesting results.

I spent nearly an hour performing a thorough analysis of Sarah Thomas' profile. It was an hour well spent. In a strange series of social media follower connections, I discovered that Sarah Thomas was Tiffany Burns' aunt. It shocked me to find a family connection between Sarah Thomas and Tiffany Burns. The two women had relationships with opposing political candidates. Did Sarah Thomas dislike Barry because he was having an affair with her niece? Or was Tiffany Burns really a spy for Wallace Bolton, using Thomas's social media feed as a smoke screen?

The whole saga became so complicated it told me it was again time to employ the whiteboard and begin mapping out the players in this soap opera. With a little luck, I might uncover more underhanded dealings that could wreck Barry McGleam's future. Maybe, with a few hours of work, I could turn the tables on my former nemesis.

THE DRAMA BEGINS AGAIN

After a few days, the urgency of Jessica's ordeal lost its importance. Even though I had done a considerable amount of work profiling the players in Jessica's life, I hadn't heard from her since the day she texted me that she was returning to Boston.

The effort I put into researching Jessica's soap opera appeared to have been a waste of time. By now, Jessica would be back home in Norfolk. She would meet with her new lawyers and lay out her path forward. There wasn't much I could do from my Berwyn location to help her.

It was best that I stayed out of her personal affairs. In Berwyn, I had a business to run. I had clients to satisfy. As I tried to put Jessica's latest saga behind me, I told myself that she was gone, and life would return to normal.

Then, a few days after Jessica returned to Norfolk, my phone dinged, signaling a text message. I hadn't heard the main phone in the front office ring, so I knew it was someone who had my private number. I feared the worst, and I was right. It was a text from Jessica. She was in trouble again.

I knew Barry's lawyers would track any communication Jessica had with others. Communication between her and me could implicate me in her proceedings. It would look as if I were undermining the prenuptial agreement between Barry and her. Barry was no dummy. He would claim Jessica was getting help from me, even claiming we were having an affair. A judge might subpoena my phone calls and texts hoping to find something steamy between Jessica and me. My privacy, and that of my clients, was in jeopardy.

If Jessica wished to communicate with me, our best option to remain undetected would be to go through an untraceable channel or one that isn't suspicious.

I had a crazy idea about how to call her. It wasn't difficult and just might work. I drove over to the Sekelsky house in my old neighborhood. They lived a few blocks away from where I grew up. The Sekelskys were model citizens and unassuming people. No one would suspect them of nefarious dealings, only concern for their daughter.

My idea was to sneak into their yard, call Jessica using their phone line, and get out without being noticed. People in Berwyn keep a keen eye open for unusual activities. Any nosy neighbor might observe my presence and tell the Sekelskys I was there. To avoid being detected, I parked in the alley behind their neighbor's house. Trying hard not to be caught doing something illegal, I rang the doorbell of the Sekelsky house to make sure nobody was home. After waiting several minutes, no one answered. I felt safe proceeding with my simple plan.

Like a lot of Berwyn residents, the Sekelskys still had a landline phone. I located the telephone protector mounted on the back wall of the house. Then, using a specially designed tool I purchased online, I tapped into Sekelsky's phone line. Making a phone call using this device would appear like the call came from a telephone inside the home. It worked. I drew a dial tone and then dialed Jessica's mobile phone number.

The caller ID would make Jessica think it was her parents calling. Even more important, anyone tracing Jessica's phone calls would also think the call came from her parents.

The phone rang twice before she answered.

The ruse worked because Jessica answered with the words, "Mom, I can't talk now. I'll call you back."

Trying to disguise my voice, I said, "Jess, it's me. Don't talk, just listen."

The line went silent.

I gave her instructions. "Go to the nearest grocery store. Buy the cheapest cellphone you can find. Use cash, no credit cards. Nothing that Barry or his lawyers can track.

"Then, using the new phone, call this number. 708-555-4682. Let me repeat. Call 708-555-4682. If you understand these instructions, confirm by pressing the number one on your keypad."

A second later, I heard the dual-tone signal from her keypad. Her confirmation told me she understood my message.

That was all. I hung up. I disconnected my makeshift wiretapping device, walked back to my car, and drove off before anyone saw me. If she followed my instructions, it would be a little while before she could get to a store and buy a new burner phone.

My mission accomplished; I headed back to my office to await her next contact. Being an expert in waiting was one of my best traits.

It took her nearly two hours. Finally, my burner phone rang. I didn't recognize the number and, as expected, the call was absent from any caller ID information. I knew it had to be Jessica calling from her new burner phone.

"Hello."

An excited Jessica cried, "Able, it's me. I need your help."

"What's happening?"

"The shit has hit the fan. I confronted Barry. I told him I was divorcing him, and I was going public with his affairs. His face turned red like a beet, and he started screaming profanities at me. He told me our marital problems were all my fault. He called me cold and prudish."

I tried to minimize her fear. "People say mean things when they are arguing."

"No, not like this. He was like a rabid dog. I brushed him off until he threatened me. He said he knows people that will take care of me. They will dump me in the Hockomock Swamp, where no one will find my body. Then he got this crazy smile on his face. I was afraid to stay in my house, so I ran out of there as fast as I could. Able, I'm scared."

"Where are you?"

"Right now, I'm hiding out at his parents' cottage in Cape Cod."

Her mention of Cape Cod triggered a memory from our past. As she spoke, my mind wandered. I remembered that besides his mansion in Norfolk, Barry's family owned several properties in the Massachusetts area. Barry liked to brag about one special place he referred to as their summer cottage, near Cape Cod. I saw the pictures of what he called a cottage. Except Barry's summer cottage was a four-bedroom brick and stone chateau on a one-acre estate overlooking the ocean. The private grounds had a manicured lawn, colorful gardens, and a saltwater pool. It was larger and more opulent than any house in my hometown of Berwyn, Illinois.

The reason I remember it was because just before Jessica and I split up, Barry invited a group of law school friends, Jessica included, to a weekend party at the cottage. He didn't include me as her plus-one on the guest list. I let Jessica know I would be unhappy if she attended without me. Despite my warning, she went anyway. She justified it as a way to make connections with other members of her chosen profession. It made me angry, but what could I do? So, I naively tried pretending it was no big deal. It was just a party.

I didn't realize it, and despite my self-denials, our relationship was probably already over. Still, I held out hope, praying Jessica would come to her senses, and realize that our love was more important than the friendship of strangers.

Jessica knew what she wanted. She wanted to be someone important, a woman of sophistication and status. I couldn't offer her those things. Only my undying love.

Jessica broke an unexpected silence. "Able, are you still there?"

"Yes, I'm sorry, I was thinking. So, you are safe?"

"No one knows I am here, but if the neighbors notice my car or the caretaker finds me here, it won't be long before Barry finds out. He'll come looking for me. I can't stay here much longer."

It was against my better judgment to leave Berwyn. Nevertheless, I knew what I was going to do. I was always willing to go out in the rain to help someone. Besides, this was Jessica. I was ready to be there if she needed help. I took a deep breath, then exhaled knowingly.

"Jess, I'm coming to get you. Keep this line clear. Don't call anyone else from this line and don't answer any calls from anyone but me. Right now, these two burner phones are the only ones we can use that are untraceable. Find a better hiding spot tonight, such as a local hotel or a B&B where they don't know you. Pay cash, no credit cards. I am heading to the airport as soon as I can book a flight. I'll be there by tomorrow."

"Hurry," she said.

* * *

Because the Chicago metropolitan area boasts quick access to two of the world's busiest airports, and it's a hub for several airlines, it offers frequent and affordable flights, exactly what I needed. It only took me ten minutes to find a direct flight to Boston, leaving the next morning at a very good price.

I hadn't been to Boston in ten years. I wasn't sure how much the area had changed.

As soon as I confirmed my flights, I texted Jessica the flight information and estimated the arrival time. That was it. The wheels were in motion for a rendezvous in Massachusetts tomorrow. I guess I will find out the details of what happened between Barry and Jessica tomorrow.

Then the weirdest thought popped into my head. In my five months of living in the Boston area, I never made it to Barry's summer cottage. Maybe tomorrow would be the day?

September 19th

Boston, Massachusetts

The Morning of the Crash

BACK TO BOSTON AND BEYOND

I woke up early Tuesday morning. I packed my carry-on bag to the gills with an extra pair of blue jeans, three casual T-shirts, and a recently pressed button-down shirt in case we went somewhere that required a collar. The weather in the Boston area was always iffy this time of year, so I brought a fleece hoodie-style sweatshirt and an extra pair of shoes. By 8:30 a.m. I was in a rideshare car heading to O'Hare Airport. I made it to the airport early, hoping the flight would be on time.

Everything went as planned. I boarded a Budget Air Boeing 737 a little after 11:00 a.m. Chicago time. Accounting for the time difference, I would be on the tarmac at Logan International Airport early that evening. Just before my plane lifted off, I texted her, "I'll grab a rental car as soon as I land. Wait for my text and let me know where you are hiding. I'll head straight there."

I put my phone in airplane mode, put my head back, and tried to remember the layout of Logan Airport. Then, as usual, a moment of sanity entered my brain. I thought, "Ābel, you must be out of your mind."

It was too late to change my mind; the plane was thundering down the runway. Against my better judgment, I was on my way to Boston to save my damsel-in-distress.

My plane landed in Boston at 6:24 p.m. As soon as I reset my phone out of airplane mode, a text popped through from Jessica. She had spent the night at an inexpensive bed & breakfast not too far from Barry's cottage on Cape Cod.

"Don't bother getting a rental car. I will pick you up at the airport," she texted.

I wasn't sure what had changed since we last spoke. She was safe but worried that Barry was looking for her. Knowing he would start his search in Cape Cod, she had to leave the area. She was driving around the Boston suburbs all day.

I wanted our rendezvous to stay as inconspicuous as possible. There was a strong likelihood that Barry would keep an eye on Jessica's whereabouts. Whomever Barry hired to find her might watch the airport terminal gates. I texted back. "Don't come into the airport. Meet me at the Hilton Hotel near the airport."

I disembarked the plane, navigated the terminal, and then caught a shuttle to the hotel. By the time I arrived at the airport Hilton, Jessica was waiting in the hotel parking lot.

I recognized her white AMG convertible. Tossing my backpack into the back seat, I instructed her to let me drive. She agreed. She climbed into the passenger seat, as I slid behind the wheel of an all-wheel drive rocket ship. The dashboard resembled something from outer space. The gauges, displays, and features of the car overwhelmed me. Back home, I drove a four-year-old Chevy Blazer.

It took me two minutes to adjust the mirrors and driver's seat position.

Before we left the airport, I asked her, "Are you okay?"

"Things have gotten worse. My phone just started blowing up. I don't know how they got my number. I haven't answered it as you instructed. Bad news. Someone just texted me that Barry's dead. The police want answers. They are looking for me."

My heart sank. It was starting again. Everywhere Jessica went, drama followed, and I always seemed to be caught in the middle of her predicament.

"Give me your phone," I instructed. Jumping out of the car, I tossed her phone as far as I could onto the grassy siding that lined the roadway that led to the hotel from the airport terminal. "If the police trace your phone, they will come here first. They will suspect you boarded a plane or at least tried; it will take anyone tracking you longer to figure it out. That might buy us some extra time."

"What are we going to do, Able?"

"I don't know. I am playing this as we go. Got any ideas?"

"We could go back to Cape Cod? It's quiet there," she said.

"I have a better idea," I said.

Instead of heading back toward Barry's Cape Cod cottage, we left the city and drove back out to the suburbs of Norfolk. I surmised I might find more answers to the news reports of Barry's murder in Jessica's hometown than in Cape Cod.

Trying to remain inconspicuous in her fancy car was going to be a challenge. Jessica's high-tech AMG likely had GPS and cellular data, which is easily trackable. I hoped the local police in Norfolk lacked the sophistication the police in larger cities might possess.

We needed the latest news on what was going down, so we stopped at a coffee shop near Dover to gain access to a Wi-Fi connection that was untraceable. I wanted to gather more information about Barry's reported death. By now, every local news channel would be all over the story. We needed to know how widespread the story had gotten.

From the latest accounts, on social media, they found Barry shot to death at his campaign headquarters in Dover, MA. The Dover Police and the Norfolk County Crime Scene Investigators estimated his time of death to be between 5:30 p.m. and 7:00 p.m.

The detectives found no weapon at the scene, and the local police were conducting interviews within the neighboring community. It mystified the police. Despite having a sophisticated security system that included a panic alert and multiple cameras, the alarm system at his office was deactivated. That told the police that Barry knew his killer.

The police spokesperson offered very few details, only suggesting there were several potential suspects still to be questioned. He stated for the record that the investigation was only beginning and was ongoing.

The crime scene investigation team revealed they found fingerprints from multiple suspects at the murder scene. Since the campaign headquarters had dozens of visitors each day, the police expected to find a lot of fingerprints.

With more than two dozen sets of prints to test, it would be hours before they could confirm a match.

I looked at Jessica. "We need to get more details on what is going on. Which way is Barry's campaign headquarters?"

Confused, she asked, "Shouldn't we be going the other way?"

"Probably, but I want to see what's happening for myself," I said.

It seemed counterintuitive to head into the action, but it was the only way to know what we were up against. We drove into Dover, intent on cruising past Barry's campaign headquarters. As I suspected, the police had cordoned the office off with crime scene tape. Police and other emergency vehicles from Dover and Norfolk County ringed the street near the entranceway. Television crews and news reporters were already assembling around the perimeter, trying to gain any tidbit of information they could inject into the breaking story. Several of Barry's campaign volunteers were onsite but appeared to be unsure how to react to this sudden turn of events. They seemed to be wondering if they should continue their duties. How much might they share with the media?

We couldn't get close to the crime scene without risking being noticed. With the news media gathering at Barry's campaign office, I presumed they would also be hawking Wallace Bolton's campaign headquarters. Our next destination was to scope out Bolton's place of business.

Bolton's offices were only about four or five miles down the road, just northeast of Barry's offices, closer to the town of Needham. As we drove, I noted that Bolton's offices were in a less affluent part of town. That told me that Barry's campaign contributions far outdrew Bolton's. It was no wonder Barry's poll numbers were higher. His campaign had the resources to outspend Bolton by a wide margin.

Just as I suspected, Bolton's headquarters buzzed with media personnel. Except that, unlike Barry's staff, Bolton's volunteers appeared to be relishing the newfound attention. Their candidate now was the front-runner. If the election went forward on schedule, Bolton would be a shoo-in to be the next District Attorney.

As we cruised past Bolton's offices, a chilling feeling overcame me. One of the beat reporters from a local news station recognized Jessica's car. As we drove past, he ran toward the street, pointing and yelling, "It's them, the murderers!" That was all I needed to hear. It was time to hightail it away from the scene and away from the action. We needed a place to lie low and stay out of sight.

Heading south out of town, we cruised out toward a rural section of the county near the Stony Brook Wildlife Area. The roads there were dark, winding, and narrow. With no traffic, we could spot anyone following us easily. It might afford us a place to go unnoticed until we figure out what to do.

Sure enough, as I suspected, the news reporter wasn't the only one to spot Jessica's car. Someone else was following us.

"We are being followed, Jess. Any idea who this is behind us?"

Jessica turned, trying to focus out the back window. The headlights in the darkness and the winding road paralleling the forest made it impossible to identify the car or driver.

Before either of us could make out the license, a dark-colored SUV rocketed up behind Jessica's car. The driver flashed their bright lights, temporarily blinding me. I held up my hand, trying to block the reflection coming off the rearview mirror.

A second later, the speeding SUV bumped the rear of Jessica's expensive AMG.

"Shit, what the hell is this asshole doing?" I exclaimed.

I wasn't about to pull over in the middle of nowhere. I hit the gas and sped up, putting some distance between the two cars. Still, the other driver pressed on, speeding up again, he reappeared behind us and this time slammed harder into the back of Jessica's AMG. This time the bump was hard enough to send our car swerving.

Once again, I tried to lose the aggressive driver, but the dark, narrow, winding road made it impossible to increase our speed safely.

As we approached a section of the roadway marked by a warning sign enforcing a twenty-mile-per-hour speed limit, I had to slow down. The other car quickly reappeared on our bumper. I had no choice but to call out to Jessica, "Hold on tight. I am going to try to lose him."

That is when it all went awry. I wasn't sure what happened, but I remember losing control of the car.

The collision with the car behind us caused Jessica's car to act erratically. I tried to regain control, but her car sped up, acting as if it had a mind of its own.

Jessica screamed, "Able, stop!" I gripped the steering wheel with all my might, trying my best to keep the vehicle in the center of the curvy roadway. The engine revved up, the tires squealed, and the steering went limp. I stomped the brakes, but the car continued accelerating. Downshifting the transmission didn't help. Nothing I did was working. Before I could regain control, everything went black.

ABLE STARTS TO REMEMBER

The next thing I remembered was staring up at a ceiling filled with bright lights. A heavyset woman and a slender young man in green hospital scrubs hovered over me. Both had their faces partially covered by masks and each was wearing surgical gloves. The woman had a stethoscope hanging from her neck.

The woman spoke first. "Welcome back Mr. Bōdyē. I am Doctor Fiedler. How are you feeling?"

It was no surprise the doctor addressed me by my proper name, Mr. Bōdyē. They must have gotten it off my driver's license.

Still dizzy and disoriented, I responded, "Ugh, terrible. What happened? Where am I?"

"This is Norfolk County Medical Center Hospital, Mr. Bōdyē. It's Wednesday, September 20th. They brought you into our emergency room late last night. You were acting erratically so we sedated you.

You've undergone quite a trauma. You've sustained a severe concussion; the collision fractured your left foot, and your wrist appears to be sprained. From what they tell me, it was quite a crash. Consider yourself lucky, no permanent damage that we can tell. I understand your friend wasn't as lucky. She is still in the ICU."

I looked around at a bevy of electronic devices with wires attached to my chest and arm. Earlier, they had inserted and taped a needle into my hand. A combination of clear liquids dripped directly into my vein through the IV.

Every part of my body ached, some parts more than others.

"I'm having a hard time breathing," I said.

"That's no surprise, your rib cage is pretty badly bruised. We are giving you a morphine drip to help with the pain. Give it a day or two and you'll start feeling better."

Glancing down, I see they encased my left foot in one of those inflatable boots to stabilize the joints. A soft cast held my left wrist and hand in place, immobilizing them.

"What time is it?" I mumbled.

The male nurse responded with. "It's half past ten. Just relax."

The doctor and nurse started a conversation between themselves, acting as if I wasn't there. After discussing their remaining tasks for the morning, they left the room, still chatting about hospital decorum. Despite having questions about Jessica, it wasn't the right time for me to ask them.

Still unsure what was happening, I lay there watching as every ten minutes, a different nurse, doctor, or medical assistant came into the room. They performed some rote tasks, then left as quickly as they came. There was even a woman who wanted to sell me an upgraded video package of newly released movies to keep me entertained as I lay there incapacitated.

Outside my hospital room, the police stationed a security guard. Not for my protection, but to keep me from trying to escape. It was ridiculous. I was in no condition to attempt a disappearance, nor did

I want to. I ached, but my bigger concern was Jessica and her condition. "What the hell happened?" I thought.

Confined to a hospital bed, I drifted in and out of a drug-induced stupor. I woke only when someone came in to check on my condition. When I was awake, I tried to piece together the events of the last few days.

* * *

Around 4:00 p.m. that afternoon, a detective from the Norfolk County Sheriff's Police appeared at my bedside.

"I am Lieutenant Hale from the Norfolk County Sheriff's Department."

Hale, a tall, muscular man with broad shoulders, brought an intimidating presence into the room. His military-style crew cut, with slightly graying temples, exudes power. He uses that power to role-play the classic bully.

Without being asked, Hale grabbed a chair and banged it down on the hard floor. Pulling a little notepad from his pocket, he sat down and hovered next to my bed.

He inquired, "How are you feeling, Mr. Body?"

"As well as can be expected."

"Can you tell me what happened the night of your accident?"

I knew Hale wasn't there to investigate the car crash. I also knew enough not to get suckered into making any statements that could implicate me or Jessica in Barry's death. Detectives like Hale skillfully manipulate suspects, extracting desired information and distorting it for greater impact.

"Another car ran us off the road. I am not a careless driver," I replied.

"I have no doubt you are an excellent driver. We looked up your driving record. I don't understand why someone would want to run you off the road. Enlighten me."

"I don't know, they just did."

"What kind of car was it, Mr. Body? The officers at the scene reported not finding any evidence of another vehicle. Your Mercedes-Benz was the only one they found at the scene. A one-car accident.

"Were you intoxicated? The officers who brought you in say you failed a field sobriety test."

I was stuck for an answer. "No… I don't know. I was injured, not drunk. It was dark. I'm not familiar with the roads in this area. From the rear-view mirror, it looked like a blue SUV."

Hale had done his homework. He knew that Jessica McGleam's presence in the same car with a man named Ābel Bōdyē, from Berwyn, Illinois, had some connection to Barry's death. He hadn't time to assemble all the pieces of the puzzle.

He tried to sound conciliatory when he said, "Mr. Body, I need your help. I am investigating the mysterious death of Barry McGleam. I think your car accident is somehow related to my case. We know you could not have killed Barry McGleam. Mr. McGleam's time of death tells us you were still in transit to Boston. We cannot say the same for Mrs. McGleam. If you know anything, tell me now. Then I won't have to charge you with obstructing justice."

"I don't know what you are talking about. Jessica is an old schoolmate. I came to Boston to reminisce about our good old university days. She told me she plans to divorce her husband. I was simply referring her to an attorney for help."

"Mr. Body, I think you are hiding something. If you are involved, we will find out what happened."

I refused to answer any more questions. "Listen, I am just telling you, a car drove us off the road. Find that other car. It might answer some of your questions."

That is when Hale became more belligerent. "I am aware you are a Private Investigator. You go by the name Able Body–Your Undercover Brother?" He snickered. "Give me a break. You seem like an intelligent man. I'm surprised that's the best you could think of."

Defending my slogan. I said, "It's a pretty good marketing scheme. My clients want an approachable guy,"

Pointing his finger directly at me, he cautioned. "Let me remind you, we do not recognize your license in the State of Massachusetts. Do not get involved in my investigation. I don't know what your part in this melodrama is, but if I find you've aided Mrs. McGleam in committing a crime. I will charge you as an accessory."

I knew from where I lay it didn't look good. Even though I committed no crime, Hale could make things miserable for me. The charges would never stick, but I didn't need the hassle.

"Right now, officer, I just want to get out of this hospital bed," I said.

"It's Lieutenant, Lieutenant Hale, and I suggest you stay where we can find you. We will talk again before you leave. Meanwhile, take some time to get your story straight."

Hale left the hospital room. He knew I wasn't telling him everything I knew about Barry's untimely death. Then again, I didn't know much.

For my part, I was concerned the police would take the path of least resistance. Jessica had the means, the motive, and likely the opportunity to kill Barry. But guys like Barry make a lot of enemies. There were several other people: Wallace Bolton, Tiffany Burns, and Sarah Thomas, who all had grudges against Barry. They all had the same means, motives, and opportunities to kill Barry as Jessica.

Would the police take the time and effort to work through all the evidence? They could just charge Jessica with the crime. Then, if Jessica dies, the police could close the case with no resistance and go back to drinking cold coffee and eating stale donuts.

I looked around the hospital room. Everyone said I was lucky to be alive. I was injured, but I was alive.

When the crash occurred, the police who were called to the scene wouldn't suspect our accident and Barry's death were somehow related. They would have treated it solely as a car accident. I needed to get out ahead of Hale's investigation. Heck, if I was healthy enough for Hale to question me, I was healthy enough to investigate the people involved. I looked around and wondered what happened to my cell phone.

My phone was in my pocket when we crashed. First, the police dragged me over half of eastern Massachusetts in that paddy wagon. Then the firefighters placed me in their ambulance and drove me to the emergency room. The emergency room attendants cut off my clothes. The crash ruined my clothes, but I had my other belongings in my backpack, along with a spare change of clothes. My phone should still be with my personal belongings.

I pressed the call button next to my bed. Seconds later, Lily, the on-duty nurse, popped back into the room.

"Lily, where is my backpack and my personal belongings?" I asked.

She looked around the room. "I don't know?"

She walked over to a storage cabinet next to the toilet doorway. "They probably put them here in this storage bin."

When she opened the cabinet. It was empty. "Hmmm," she said. "The staff downstairs in the emergency room usually tags them and makes sure they get placed in your room when they admit you to the main part of the hospital. You were unconscious when the paramedics brought you downstairs. They were all probably too busy to ask. I'll have to check and see if there is any record."

Adding to my problems, I had to deal with the police. I had no phone, no way to contact anyone for help, and I was bound to a hospital bed without enough strength to make a stink.

CALLING RALPH DOWDEN

The next morning, I was more alert. They brought me a breakfast of oatmeal, toast, and a cup of apple juice. The oatmeal tasted like paste, so I dumped some of the apple juice into the bowl to give it some flavor. The toast was cold, but I ate it anyway. As I slurped the last of my juice, an orderly came in with my overnight bag.

"We found it," he said. "Apparently, the police returned it after they sent you from the emergency room up here to room 308. Looks like your wallet, laptop, and cellphone are inside. There are some clothes in here, too."

I examined the contents. Everything was there. Somehow, my bag took a detour from the emergency room to the police station before being delivered back to the hospital. When Lieutenant Hale found out his primary suspect, Jessica McGleam, was involved in a car crash, he started asking questions. Learning I was with her, Hale put two and two together and confiscated my bag. In Massachusetts, probable cause alone is insufficient for him to inspect my belongings. He must have evidence of a crime. To me, Hale was overstepping his bounds.

It filled my mind with questions. How did Hale tie the car crash and Barry's death together so quickly? Did Hale or the Norfolk

County CSI team illegally examine my belongings? Did they have a search warrant?

I have enough experience to know an unwarranted search is my get-out-of-jail-free card. If Hale fancied any charges against me, a talented lawyer would have a field day getting them dismissed.

I concluded Hale knew I could not have killed McGleam. I wasn't being held. Instead, Hale was probably hoping I would give him some evidence that implicated Jessica McGleam. I'm a free man, for now. Everything hinged on Jessica's recovery. Still, I wondered. "How much did Hale know?"

* * *

Lieutenant Hale warned me to stay out of his investigation. That would not happen. No one, especially the police, knew the history of events as well as me. Jessica, the only other one capable of recounting the past few weeks, remained in a medically induced coma. For the first time since becoming a private investigator, Able Body - Your Undercover Brother had his very own actual murder mystery to solve. If I cracked this murder case, all those people who laughed at my funny name would eat their words. I wouldn't have to go back to taking pictures of cheating wives and wayward husbands. I would be a real detective, charging big money to necessitous clients.

* * *

I still had a hard time accepting that I had lost control of Jessica's car. Something or someone caused that car's rapid acceleration.

Hale dismissed my claim that the accident and murder were related.

The police, the District Attorneys, and the other lawyers were preoccupied with arguing over procedural issues and who to charge in Barry McGleam's death. Nobody was looking for additional evidence beyond the original crime scene.

While in the hospital, I came up with a plan to piece together the events since Jessica's visit to my office in Berwyn. I knew I couldn't do it without help. I had my cell phone back; I could contact the outside world. But who could I trust? There was only one person I trusted implicitly. As soon as I could get some privacy, I placed a call back home to Thelma Jenkins.

"Mr. Body, I have been so worried about you. Where are you?" asked Thelma.

"I am in the Norfolk County Medical Center Hospital. I was involved in a car accident. They tell me I am going to be okay. But I need your help."

"Is this about that woman? The one who called but wouldn't leave a name? I know you have the case plotted out on the whiteboard in your office. I had a feeling she would cause trouble."

"Yes, her name is Jessica McGleam. She's an old girlfriend of mine. Her maiden name is Sekelsky. We went to high school together in Berwyn. The accident also injured her. I'm relying on you to be my eyes and ears for the next few days. A crucial investigation is happening here in the Boston area. She needs me to be involved. I don't have all the facts, but the next few days are critical. I will catch you up when I know more. Clear my calendar and stay near the phone. Oh, and get a message to my parents. Don't alarm them, just let them know I will be out of contact for a few more days."

"Yes Sir, Mr. Body. I will call them right away. I'll be here if you need me. Call anytime."

Thelma was the most reliable person I knew. I reminded myself if I get through this drama with Jessica unscathed to give Thelma a raise.

With Thelma handling the coordination of evidence, I looked for help in the Norfolk County area. My broken foot was going to make snooping around a lot more difficult. It wasn't easy moving around with your foot in a cast. Being inconspicuous would be problematic. Witnesses will remember a guy on crutches. I needed someone to help me, who could maintain a low profile.

After contemplating for a few minutes, an idea struck me. My old boss and mentor, Ralph Dowden, came to mind. Ralph is likely in his seventies at this point. He's not the ideal candidate to work on a murder investigation, but his investigation wouldn't raise a lot of suspicions. And, if Ralph still held his license in Massachusetts, it would solve a litany of legal stumbling blocks.

It only took me five minutes to find a phone number for Ralph Dowden. With limited optimism, I dialed the number. To my surprise, someone answered on the second ring.

"Hello, this is Ralph Dowden. How may I help you?"

"Ralph Dowden, this is Ābel Bōdyē. I hope you remember me. Around ten years ago, during my college years, I completed some computer work for you. I called you a few years ago for advice."

"Bōdyē? I don't think so. You say you worked for me?"

After a few seconds, it clicked. "Oh yeah, BODY. Able Body, I remember. I loved that name. What can I do for you after all these years?"

Even though the public knew me as Able Body, I hated it when people who knew better called me Able Body. It was like fingernails on a chalkboard.

"I need a private investigator. Are you still working?"

"Well, I am what you might call semi-retired. I still do people searches when the opportunity presents itself. I don't do surveillance or undercover any longer. I primarily work from home on the computer. What's this about?"

I started my sales pitch. "How would you like to earn some extra cash? I need a local man in the Boston area. Nothing you can't handle. I'll take the lead."

"I am going to need more information. Tell me more."

"This is hard to explain, but I am hoping you will meet with me at Norfolk County Medical Center Hospital, room 308. I broke my foot in a car accident. I had a concussion. The hospital won't release me for a few more days. If we can meet, I can explain the entire story to you in confidence."

"Hold on. Let me write this down. Norfolk County Medical Center Hospital, room 308. I'm free this afternoon. I will be there within a couple of hours."

Telling Ralph I was in the hospital with a broken foot was a tricky way to entice him. It implied a case of simple negligence or some sort of injury settlement. Little did he know that signing on to help me would involve him in a blockbuster murder investigation.

Ralph hung up, and I buzzed for the nurse on duty. She came surprisingly quickly. I think she was right outside my room.

"Can you get me a pad of paper and a couple of pens? I need to catch up on my writing," I asked.

Just as I ended my conversation with Ralph, the phone rang once again. The Caller ID told me it was my parents. They must have received Thelma's message. As expected, they were worried.

I tried my best to sound chipper. "Hello, Mom and Dad."

A sweet voice, tendered with a slight Slavic accent, spoke first. "Able, it's Mom. Are you all right?"

"Yes, Mom, I just had a little accident. My foot is broken."

I didn't tell her about lying in a jail cell spewing blood from my mouth, being brought into the emergency room by a fire department ambulance, the concussion, or the bruised ribs.

"Oh, honey, what can we do?"

I was talking to my mom, but I knew my dad was listening in. He piped in, "What the hell are you doing in Boston? Are you back chasing that Sekelsky girl again?"

Despite my being thirty-two years old, he still growled when I did something he didn't agree with.

"This is work, Dad. I am on a case."

Rather than start an argument between my dad and me, my mom interjected. "Honey, do you need us to come to Boston?"

"No, Mom, everything is okay. I will be home in a few days. I'll call you with an update when I know more."

My dad piped in again. "Finish what you are doing and come home."

I signed off, promising to finish my work and return to Illinois, ASAP. The context of the call explained why I asked Thelma to contact them. I wanted to avoid the parental dialogue that just occurred.

A few short minutes after I hung up with my parents, a pretty young orderly named Lily brought me a yellow legal pad of paper and a blue, black, and red ballpoint pen. "Will these work for you, Sir?"

"Yes, Lilly. These will be perfect."

I began by drawing a line down the middle of the page, making two lists. On the left side, I wrote Bad Guys, and on the right Good Guys. The Good Guy's side was easy. I wrote my name, Thelma Jenkins, and Ralph Dowden. On the Bad Guy's side, I wrote Barry McGleam, Tiffany Burns, and Sarah Thomas.

I debated which side the next two names should appear on, Jessica Sekelsky-McGleam and Lieutenant Hale. I put down the pen, realizing it was too early to assign suspicion to anyone. My investigation was just starting, but at least I was on my way. Soon, I would have a mountain of evidence to share with Lieutenant Hale.

IN THE CLEAR - FOR NOW

When Lieutenant Hale left the hospital yesterday, he also withdrew the security guard who was stationed outside my hospital room. I guess he realized I wasn't a flight risk. As long as I stayed out of Hale's way, I was in the clear.

The hospital attendant brought dinner to my room around 5:00 p.m. It was earlier than I normally ate my dinner, but I was hungry, and the food was tolerable. Halfway through my petite servings of bland chicken teriyaki and steamed green beans, a gray-haired gentleman with pasty white skin walked into the room. It was Ralph Dowden.

Ralph looked considerably older than when I remembered him, nearly ten years ago. Never a big man, he seemed even smaller than when we last worked together. His arms and legs resembled sticks and his belly hung over his belt loops. The ten years that passed turned Ralph into the Incredible Shrinking Man. It made me wonder what his mental capacity would be like. Was he still the no-nonsense guy I remember? Would he still be able to comprehend the complicated situation Jessica and I faced?

Ralph extended his hand. With my left hand immobilized, I reached across the bed, extending my right hand. "Forgive me, my left hand is still a little sore," I said.

"Looks like you had some misfortune. Is that what this is all about? Your accident?"

"Yes and no," I replied. "I think you'd better sit down. I have a lot to tell you."

He walked around the room and pulled a chair from near the window, to a spot closer to my bed.

"Do you read the papers, Ralph?" I asked.

"I read them online. I've become much more adept with computers over the past few years. In this business, it's important to keep up with the latest trends. Besides, I can't afford to hire a young college guy to research the internet like I did when you worked for me."

I liked what I heard. Ralph's remarks meant he remembered me from our past association. It also meant that if Ralph was keeping up with technology, he could be helpful.

"Are you familiar with the recent death of Norfolk County District Attorney candidate Barry McGleam?" I asked.

"Yeah, I read about it. Some kind of love triangle gone bad. They think his ex-wife did it. The cops are looking for her. Nasty stuff."

"Well, you haven't gotten the whole story. Yeah, Barry was screwing around, but I don't think his wife did it. I think it could have been someone else trying to frame her."

"Why would you think that? What is your involvement in this affair?" asked Ralph.

"Sit back and relax. It's a long story. I think you may find it interesting."

Ralph had driven down from Natick to meet with me based on my phone call. He had nowhere else to go. "Okay, I am all ears."

"Ten years ago, I was on a waiting list to enter Northeastern University's law program. That is when I started working for you. The woman I was dating, Jessica Sekelsky, dumped me for Barry McGleam, our dead man. Since I didn't get accepted to

Northeastern, I returned to Illinois from Boston. A few years later, Jessica became McGleam's wife. She chose the right path because Barry became rich and successful.

"Meanwhile, I was trying my hand at several careers, hoping to find something that fit my personality. I wasn't finding my niche until I remembered you, Ralph Dowden, and the work you did. You seemed to be happy and pretty successful, so eventually, I followed in your footsteps. I became a Private Investigator, in Illinois."

"Yes, I remember you called me once asking about insurance jobs," Ralph said. "You started your own firm. You came up with that goofy name, *Able Body–Your Undercover Brother*." Ralph shook his head. "Seriously, was that the best name you could think of for a professional agency?"

As usual, I defended my marketing decision. "Hey, I was trying to come up with a marketing plan. I figured since everyone calls me Able Body anyway, I might as well use it to my advantage. Besides, it seems to have been a good idea. People remember the name Able Body."

Ralph shook his head again. "You think Jessica is innocent? That it's a frame job."

"Correct," I said. "Anyway, Jessica and Barry's marriage was on the rocks. About two weeks ago, she contacted me for help. I referred her to an attorney here in the Boston area who specializes in nasty divorce situations. Her new attorney challenged Barry. That's when the shit hit the fan. The ranker escalated to threats of violence.

"I thought I was done, but Jessica has a knack for drawing me into her life. She needs my help.

"Barry was running for office as the Norfolk County District Attorney. He was also playing around with a girl named Tiffany Burns. Tiffany is an exotic dancer over at the Peppermint Club. Jessica threatened to expose Barry's affair and cause a scandal. He couldn't let a scandal ruin his election chances at the last minute.

"This is where it gets twisted. Tiffany is the niece of a woman named Sarah Thomas, who, coincidentally, is the live-in girlfriend of McGleam's biggest opponent Wallace Bolton."

"Sounds like a soap opera," replied Ralph.

"It is. The number of related incidents suggests that this is more than just bad luck. The police are taking the fast track. They believe it is a simple revenge motive. Most often, these are crimes of passion. They are playing the percentages. Suspecting the spouse as the guilty party."

"They are usually right," Ralph replied.

"Wait, there's more. The wife, Jessica Sekelsky-McGleam, is upstairs in the ICU. She was in the same near-fatal car crash that put me in here. She may or may not pull through. I was driving the car with Jessica in the passenger seat when we crashed. The police refused to believe me, but we were driven off the road by another car.

"I believe the person who caused the accident is also the one responsible for Barry McGleam's murder. I think they were trying to kill Jessica. The police would naturally focus on the wife as the primary suspect. Especially since Barry's affair would come out in the open. If Jessica couldn't talk or defend herself, the police would close the case as a domestic squabble. It would be a pseudo-murder-suicide. No one counted on me being there or that Jessica and I might survive.”

“Wow, that’s some complex story. Can you prove any of your claims?” asked Ralph.

“That’s what I aim to do. I began assembling a pretty comprehensive preliminary investigation before I came to Norfolk. I need your help to do some deeper investigation and evidence gathering. Since my license isn’t recognized here, I can’t go digging around like I would like to.”

Ralph shook his head. I still hadn’t sold him on the idea of helping me. “I have done nothing this complicated in years. I think you might be better off finding a younger, faster investigator. My skills aren’t what they used to be. Mostly, I stay in my home office. I have spent the last two years writing my memoir.”

I argued, “You just told me you like to keep up with the latest trends. This may be your most significant case in years. It could be your crowning achievement to a lifelong career.”

He shook his head. “Possibly the last laugh of a washed-up investigator. Why don’t you let me find you another detective? A more fitting option.”

Standing up, Ralph reached out his hand. “I’ll get back to you in a day or two. Meanwhile, you work on getting better. These things tend to resolve themselves, so don’t worry.”

I wasn’t ready to give up. I implored Ralph. “What more can I do to convince you to help, Ralph?”

“I’ll get back to you in a day or two,” he repeated. He turned and exited the hospital room.

I had just hit my first roadblock. My plan wasn't working as easily as I hoped. Hiring a private investigator gets expensive really fast. I should know. I still had Thelma back in Illinois, but I needed someone here in Massachusetts. Someone I could trust. I didn't want to start over with someone I didn't know.

TOO SOON TO RETIRE

The next morning, fortune shined down on me once again. My phone rang. It was a call from Ralph Dowden. I was fully expecting Ralph to offer me several names of younger investigators to contact for help. Instead, overnight, he reconsidered my proposal.

"On my way home yesterday, I thought about your situation. I may be an old man, Body, but I'm not ready to hang up my credentials. Solving an unexplained death could be my last act of defiance to Father Time. If we succeed, it will be a great last chapter to my memoir."

He paused for a second, then said, "I'm in. Tell me what you want me to do."

I was ecstatic. "Ralph, that's great," I replied. "I already have a preliminary investigation started. I will have my secretary send you a copy. The doctors are telling me as soon as I can walk on my own without assistance, they will release me from this hospital. I won't be able to drive for a couple of days, so I will have to arrange other transportation.

"We can stay in communication by phone until I know more. The first chance we get, let's meet and discuss everything I know and the next steps. I'll call you tomorrow as soon as I have a better timeline."

"Listen, young man, when you know you'll be released, call me. I'll swing by the hospital to pick you up. We can work together out of my home office," said Ralph.

"Ralph, you're a lifesaver. Check your email in a little while. I am going to have my assistant send you copies of the files I have."

As soon as I hung up, I dialed my office phone, hoping to catch Thelma Jenkins at her desk. "Thelma, it's Able. I got a job for you."

"Yes, Mr. Body, what can I do?"

"You know that file we have been working on for Jessica Sekelsky?" Even after a decade, I couldn't break the habit of calling her by her maiden name. Deep inside, I still could not accept her marriage to Barry McGleam. To me, she will always be Jessica Belle Sekelsky.

"Yes," she replied.

"Make a digital copy of the entire file. Then take some pictures of the whiteboard. Forward a copy of everything to Ralph Dowden in Natick, MA. You'll find his email on my computer's contact list. Send me a courtesy copy so I can see what we have."

"Consider it done," she said.

"Oh, and stand by. I am going to need you to do some additional research."

"Yes, sir, I will."

Upon hanging up with Thelma, my mood soared. I now had a reliable team to help me uncover the truth behind Barry McGleam's death and the car accident that injured me and may have fatally harmed Jessica.

I was ready to get to work. All I needed now was to get out of the hospital and find a place to stay and work for a few days.

I didn't sleep well that night. It wasn't the pain that kept me awake; it was the excitement of undertaking this important investigation. I wanted to prove Lieutenant Hale wrong. But mostly I wanted to find the person who ran us off the road and nearly killed Jessica and me. If we somehow stumbled onto Barry McGleam's killer, so be it.

ABLE BODY RETURNS

On the third day in the hospital, my mobility significantly improved. The headache from my concussion was gone. I still had some soreness in my ribs, but it wasn't bad enough to keep me in bed. The nurses helped me sit up in a chair and, with the help of a medical assistant; I was using the bathroom. With less pain, I reduced the pain medications the nurses were giving me, and my mind was clearing. The physical therapist that the hospital assigned to me advised me to move around more to get my muscles working. He recommended using one of those wheelie scooters that you kneel on to keep the weight off of my shattered foot while I cruised up and down the halls. The scooter was too cumbersome to maneuver. I kept bumping into things and almost fell off a couple of times, turning a corner. Instead, I opted for a pair of old-fashioned crutches. With practice, on crutches, I could match the speed of someone with two healthy legs.

With my crutches, I was moving around better, and the nurse encouraged me to get some exercise pending my release. As soon as I could move around without an escort, I hobbled to the elevator that took me upstairs to the Intensive Care Unit where Jessica was still in a medically induced coma. I peered through the glass wall to see my once beautiful girlfriend lying there, broken. She had tubes and wires of all types attached to her body and a ventilator tube was doing her breathing.

When I questioned the nurse at the desk outside the ICU about her condition, I received a practiced response. "Are you a relative?"

"No, I am a friend. My name is Ābel Bōdyē. Mrs. McGleam and I were together the night of her accident. I am a patient in room 308 downstairs. I need to know her condition."

"I'm sorry sir, but I can only give that information to a relative or someone legally allowed on her behalf."

The nurse gave me a serious look. She shook her head as if to indicate Jessica's prognosis was negative. Then she folded her hands in a praying motion. Her actions told me all I needed to know. The doctors and nurses were doing all they could. Jessica was in God's hands now.

I'm not a religious person. I haven't prayed much in recent years. Prayer never seemed to work for me. Later that night, when the hospital got quiet, I tried to remember some prayers my parents had taught me as a boy. It certainly couldn't hurt.

The rest of my day was spent surfing the internet, trying to learn everything I could about Barry's death, the car accident, and the police investigation. When I wasn't on the computer, I practiced moving around on crutches. To be a detective, I needed to move around unencumbered.

RALPH AND ABLE – PARTNERS

I hung around all the next morning for the doctor to release me. They finally gave me a decent breakfast of eggs, turkey sausage, and hot coffee. It helped me pass the time. I couldn't wait to get out of this hospital and start our investigation. Just before 11:00 a.m., the doctor sauntered into my room.

"How are you feeling, Mr. Bōdyē? That gash on your head still looks pretty nasty."

The doctor examined the stitches and then asked, "How's the wrist?"

"It's okay, doc. Really, I think you have done all you can. I believe it's time for me to reenter the world.

After a cursory exam, the doctor agreed. "I think you are good to go. But let me caution you to take it easy. No strenuous activities for another week. Get lots of rest. You're still in recovery."

"Okay, Doctor. I'll be good," I promised.

Before I left the hospital, I bounced my way upstairs to the ICU to check on Jessica. I couldn't enter the room, but I could at least check on her condition through the glass partition near the nurses' station.

Opposite the ICU entrance, the hospital maintained a small waiting area furnished with four chairs and a loveseat. As I approached the entry to the ICU, I noticed an elderly couple seated on the loveseat. It took a few seconds for it to register, but I knew them. Jessica's parents, George and Marian Sekelsky, were there in the waiting area.

"Mr. and Mrs. Sekelsky?" I queried.

The woman gasped. "Oh." The man looked up, startled.

"Oh, Able," she said. "I didn't expect to see you here."

That is when the dam broke. All the emotions I held inside came bursting out. I broke down in tears. "Mrs. Sekelsky, I am so sorry this happened. I was with Jessica when the crash happened. I'm sorry, I couldn't protect her."

"What the hell happened out there?" snapped George Sekelsky.

"I was trying to help Jessica. She is getting blamed for Barry's death. I believe she is not involved in it."

Marian Sekelsky placed her hand on my cheek and wiped a tear from my eye. "Oh, Able, please don't blame yourself. It was an accident. Look at you. Your head, your foot. You're hurt."

"I should have stayed out of it. She wouldn't be in there now, lying there with tubes and wires keeping her alive."

Marian Sekelsky smiled a sad smile. "Able, I always wished you and Jessica had gotten married. She loved you. It always bothered me she chose money and prestige over true love."

"I loved her," I bellowed. "I still love her. More than anything else."

I looked at George. "Mr. Sekelsky, I promise you I will find out what happened. I will clear Jessica's name."

Then something happened that surprised me. George Sekelsky wrapped his arms around me and hugged me.

"I'm sorry I snapped at you, son. I know this wasn't your fault. We're here to take care of Jessica. When this is over, you are welcome in our home anytime."

I took a seat next to the Sekelskys and waited with them, exchanging small talk about the old neighborhood and my parents. About forty-five minutes after I arrived, the ICU nurse interrupted. "The doctor will try to wean Jessica off the ventilator and assess her ability to breathe independently. If you would like to come inside, she can use your support."

"Can I come too?" I asked.

"Yes, Able, please. Jessica wants you there. I know she does," said Marian.

We entered the ICU room where Jessica lay with a dozen wires and tubes attached to her body. Her legs and feet were bandaged to treat the burns she sustained from the fiery crash.

A heart monitor beeped away in rhythm like a smoke alarm that needed its battery replaced. Every five seconds, a whoosh from a ventilator filled her lungs and then let them deflate naturally, bringing healing oxygen into her body.

The doctor turned towards the Sekelskys. "She has been in a medically induced coma for several days because of the swelling of her brain. The swelling is decreasing. We are bringing her out of her comatose state. She is still heavily sedated, but we hope for her to breathe on her own if possible. This is a big step. Please stay calm."

Together, the doctor and the nurse waited for the device to fill her lungs one more time, then he gently pulled the long narrow tube from her throat and let her lungs deflate naturally. Everyone watched and waited. A few seconds later, she took a shallow breath on her own. The heart monitor beeped erratically as her body fought to gain control. Then another breath, and another until they became stronger and more consistent. The heart monitor resumed its steady beep, beep, beep.

Relief came across the doctor's face. "Good girl, Jessica," he said.

Tears streamed from George and Marian's eyes.

The doctor glanced at Jessica, who was still lying there sedated. "We're not in the clear, but this is a significant step forward. Keep praying for your daughter. She is strong, and she wants to live. We will do everything in our power to make it happen."

We stood there watching Jessica breathe, half hoping she would awaken and all would be well. She continued to lie there in a medicated stupor.

A few minutes later, I felt my phone buzz. "Excuse me."

It was Ralph Dowden. He was downstairs, waiting. Although I wanted to spend more time with Jessica, I couldn't delay the investigation any further.

"Mr. and Mrs. Sekelsky, I have to leave. I will be back as soon as possible." I handed George my business card. "Please call me if anything changes or you need my help."

I maneuvered myself between the machines and wires that were keeping Jessica alive and placed a kiss on her head. "I'll be back soon, sweetheart."

Ambling on my crutches as quickly as possible, I made my way to the front of the building. There was Ralph in a silver compact SUV.

I tossed my backpack and crutches into Ralph's back seat and hobbled into the passenger seat next to Ralph.

"Thank you again for coming to get me, Ralph. I have good news. Jessica is off the ventilator. She's beginning to recover."

"That's wonderful news. I wish her well," said Ralph.

* * *

Ralph put the car in gear and headed north along Rte. 155. It was a fifteen-mile trip to our destination, the town of Natick and Ralph's home office. Both of us had doubts regarding the dynamics of this new partnership. Limited because my injuries prevented me from driving, my investigation was at the mercy of Ralph's energy level. I wanted to act fast, but without Ralph's help, my investigation was going nowhere.

Lieutenant Hale already warned me to keep my nose out of his investigation. Since they did not recognize my license in Massachusetts, Ralph would be the lead guy in whatever digging we did.

We drove on for a few minutes. I finally broke the silence. "What's the plan?"

"We are going back to my house. We can work out of my home office. I'll help you set up your computer and get you oriented on how we do things around here. I have already received the files from your secretary via email. We can start by reviewing them."

I stared out the window, trying to orient myself to the Norfolk County area. I watched as Ralph turned off Rte. 155 and onto Rte. 27 North. Ralph's house was at the north end of town. His home was an older turn-of-the-century Cape Cod-style building on a block with other quaint, well-maintained bungalows and cottages. Clad with pale blue wood siding and white gingerbread trim, it looked like a page out of Better Homes and Gardens.

Ralph pulled into the driveway that extended to the rear of the property and a garage painted to match the house. He stopped short at a brick walkway that led to three steps and a small porch. Hopping out of the car, I grabbed my crutches from the back seat. Ralph secured my bag and guided me up the stairs to his front door. He opened the door and in a courteous tone said, "Please come in."

Stepping inside, I looked around. The house, recently renovated, had a mix of old-world charm and modern practicality. "Nice place," I commented.

"You can thank my wife. Building and maintaining the house was her responsibility. I was working all the time. Mostly in the city."

"She did a great job."

Ralph asked. "Are you hungry? You must be tired of that hospital food. I made some pretty good chili, not too spicy. I can warm up a couple of bowls."

"Sounds great. I haven't had homemade food in days," I replied.

Pointing towards the room on the left. Ralph instructed, "Put your stuff in that room."

I peeked ahead and saw a den that he transformed into a large office space. The inside of the office surprised me. I saw a well-equipped room with two large oak desks facing each other. Each desk had a computer monitor, a mouse, and a docking station where someone with a laptop computer could connect with ease. Along the wall were a row of matching file cabinets and a stand-alone multi-function printer that worked as a scanner, copier, and fax machine.

Above the printer hung a familiar memory. There was the framed poster I remembered from when I worked at Ralph's old office ten years ago. I smiled when I read the inscription. "We all deserve justice. Most people can't afford it." That single piece of artwork reminded me of why I entered this business.

The desk furthest from the door had a computer monitor and laptop. The laptop was powered up and ready to start working. "That must be Ralph's primary workstation." I thought. He had already printed a copy of my preliminary report, which he spread about the desktop. I noticed several notations Ralph had already made to the text.

I pulled my laptop from my backpack and connected it to the docking station on the desk opposite Ralph's. I hit the power button and watched as it booted up, waiting to connect to the network.

"What's the Wi-Fi password?" I called out to Ralph.

"Never mind that now. The chili's ready. Come and eat. I'll help you get online after lunch."

Ralph and I sat at a vintage kitchen table. The oak finish showed spots of wear at the edges where people had rested their arms while eating. Over the years, scratches and dents accumulated from dropped or banged cutlery and dishes. Despite being worn, the chairs were sturdy and well-crafted. They reflected Ralph Dowden's character, comfortable and unpretentious.

As we sat across from each other scooping spoonsful of Ralph's homemade chili and oyster crackers into our mouths, we chatted.

The focus wasn't on work but on ourselves and our lives. Between mouthfuls, Ralph talked about how his life had transpired these last ten years since I worked for him as an intern.

"I've seen a lot of changes in the last few years. I don't know if you remember, but I retired from the insurance business with a nice pension. Then, when I embarked on my small business, I thought I had everything I needed for the rest of my life. It was all going to be gravy. Four years ago, they diagnosed my wife with terminal cancer. I wanted to help care for her, so I closed my office and stepped away from investigations. I kept my license active, hoping she would recover, and I could go back to work. She fought hard for a year, but the doctors couldn't cure her. She died three years ago.

"There was no reason to retire to a rocking chair in my den. I wanted to keep busy, so I took a few computer classes. Then I furnished this new office here at home with the latest technology. Since I had little else to do, I opted to write a book detailing my investigations and experiences. I began with great enthusiasm but eventually ran out of stories. I never finished the book. The last chapter eluded me.

"After a few months of sitting here in the office, I started calling some of my past clients. Most of them had already found other agencies, but I picked up a job here and there. Nothing as big as wrongful death, just a few missing persons or an insurance investigation. Working has helped keep me relevant."

"I'm sorry to hear about your wife. Being alone kinda sucks. I guess that's something we have in common. Chili's good."

"How long are you staying here in Boston?" Ralph asked.

"As long as it takes to sort this whole mess out. Regardless of what happens, I am committed to seeing it through to the end."

"Where are you staying tonight?"

"I don't know. I guess I need to check into a motel or something. Got any recommendations?"

"You might as well stay here. At least until you can drive again. I got two guest rooms that nobody ever uses." Then he laughed. "If you can stand to eat chili two or three times a week."

"Well, if I rent an automatic transmission car, I can drive again. My right foot is okay, and my wrist is feeling pretty good."

Again, he stepped up. "Don't push it. At least wait until you get off those crutches. I can drive you anywhere you need to go."

Ralph's generosity took me aback. Ralph didn't owe me anything. I took a deep breath, then let out a sigh of relief. Between myself, Thelma, and Ralph, my optimism for getting my life back on track toward success was growing. Maybe the dark clouds that have been hovering over me, blocking my vision, all these years were dissipating?

"Okay, Ralph. I am gonna take you up on that offer. I promise I won't be a bother. Although I don't cook, I can either order pizza for dinner or make oatmeal for breakfast occasionally. Maybe we can grill up a steak and baked potatoes."

Ralph looked back and nodded. "It's a deal."

While Ralph cleaned up the dishes from lunch, I hobbled back to the office. I fiddled with my laptop computer and waited for my new partner. While I waited, I glanced over at Ralph's desk. Ralph was already working on the files he had received from Thelma

Jenkins. He had made several notations – items of interest – that he felt needed additional explanation.

Ralph returned to his office to see me sitting there, anxiously waiting for him to give me the Wi-Fi password.

"You didn't have to wait. Let me show you a little trick to get around the password."

He pointed to the shelf along the wall where an internet router sat flashing with yellow and green data streams.

"Go over to the router and push the button labeled WPS. It will flash. Then quickly go into the settings on your phone or computer and search for the Wi-Fi network. Mine is called, 'DowdenAgency5.0'. Select that network and it will connect your device without using the password."

Ralph watched me walk over to the router. I located and depressed the WPS button on the front panel. It flashed, blinking like a warning sign at the side of a construction site. Then Ralph pointed toward me. "Now," he said.

I located the Wi-Fi network in my laptop's network settings, clicked the mouse, and instantly it connected.

"I'm connected! I've never considered doing that," I exclaimed.

"I took a computer class a few years ago. I learned lots of neat stuff. Remember it. It may come in handy someday."

We had only been working together again for one hour and already the old veteran had taught me a new trick to add to my skill set. Not only was this partnership going to help me find out who killed Barry McGleam, but it may keep me out of jail while we searched for clues.

"To make everything legal, I'll hire you as a consultant. Invoice me for your time at two hundred dollars a day. List your expenses on a separate line item. In return, I'll pay for your time charging you two hundred a day for your room. I'll reimburse your expenses by charging you for your meals. This way the I.R.S. won't complain and if the police bother you, it is all above board."

Ralph knew how to play the game. Our new partnership appeared both practical and lawful.

Though it was early, the long day had already worn me out. The doctors, the Sekelskys, and the planning of our strategy took its toll. Ralph could see I was tired.

"Let me show you to your room and get you settled in," he said. "We can hit this investigation hard in the morning. I work best after a good night's sleep."

I welcomed the opportunity to relax without the noise and commotion of the hospital.

Ralph's guest room was quaint and comfortable. The room appeared untouched for years. It was as if it were waiting for me. I unpacked my bag. Turned down the bedspread, laid my head on a soft feather pillow and in minutes I was sound asleep.

DOWDEN'S HOME SWEET HOME

I woke up early the next morning to the smell of freshly brewed coffee. It was still dark outside, but Ralph was already busying about. I showered quickly, put on my last set of clean blue jeans and a burgundy T-shirt, and headed downstairs.

By the time I walked into the kitchen, Ralph had defrosted some banana-nut muffins and had the coffee ready to pour.

"How do you take it?" he asked.

"Hot and black," came my reply.

"I figured as much. When I was sitting behind the wheel of an automobile, doing overnight surveillance, there was no time for fancy drinks. I drank coffee, black, and lots of it. If I had to pee it went in an empty milk jug."

We gobbled down our muffins, refilled our coffee mugs, and headed to the office. Time was wasting.

Ralph sat down opposite me and then shuffled through the pile of papers on his desk. He grabbed a pencil from a desk drawer and started going through the list.

"Okay, let's talk about each one of these people on your list. I want to start with the most basic question. Which one of these people had the motive to kill Barry McGleam?"

My new partner and I navigated down the list, starting with Barry's political opponent, Wallace Bolton.

Ralph summarized his thoughts on Bolton. "He definitely had a powerful motive. Barry's death brings a lot of publicity to this District Attorney election. That means a lot of free publicity for Bolton. With Barry out of the way, it would help his chances of getting elected."

Ralph continued his theory, "Of course, he had to know the Governor might appoint someone temporarily, and then call for a new election. Maybe he thinks he has a better chance against another candidate?"

Ralph made some good points. I went next, looking at the profile of Tiffany Burns as the villain. "I like her for the crime. If Barry had just used her and dumped her or even threatened her, she may have taken her revenge. Plus, she's an exotic dancer. She probably knows a lot of shady people. The men who frequent her club would be happy to help her out, especially if they think she will pay them with special favors. I would bet Tiffany had easy access to a gun. She's my top suspect."

Ralph took his turn, going down the list to Wallace Bolton's girlfriend. "Then there's this one, Sarah Thomas. I don't think she has a strong enough motive. It's hard to imagine her loyalty to Bolton would extend to murder. I think she is our least likely suspect."

An uneasy silence fell across the room. The one suspect that I refused to acknowledge was Jessica. Ralph wasn't afraid to examine Jessica's involvement. He broke the silence.

"Now we have your girlfriend, Jessica. She has motives, lots of them. A cheating spouse who threatened to kill her and hide her body in a swamp. She had the means to do it. She had free access to McGleam's home and offices. Her whereabouts during the murder are unknown. From my viewpoint, she has no alibi. It is no surprise the police are targeting her."

"I know Ralph. It doesn't look good. She said she didn't do it. My second sense tells me she isn't lying. The timing of it is too close. She was on her way to the airport to meet me when someone else shot Barry. I am still trying to tie our accident to this whole affair. I am telling you someone tried to kill Jessica and take me along as collateral damage."

Ralph explained. "There is one more possibility we can add to this list. In Massachusetts, if a candidate wins the election but cannot take office, another candidate chosen by a committee can fill his position. Is it possible that McGleam's party members expected him to win the election post-mortem? They wanted to win the election. Maybe they didn't want him in office after the election?"

"I suppose that is possible, but that's a pretty big stretch. Barry McGleam was a lawyer who prosecuted criminals and was good at his job. He was your typical sleazy politician. The fact that he was a womanizer who frequented gentlemen's clubs seemed to have no bearing on his electability. We can't account for every conspiracy theory. The number of his enemies could be limitless. I think the list of people who actually would kill him is shorter. Let's keep the list manageable, for now."

Ralph agreed. "Yeah, you're probably right. This is a good starting point but we're gonna need more current data. We need to concentrate on means and opportunity. Maybe we can cross one or two off your list.

"I have a friend, Nancy Klein, who works at the Norfolk County district attorney's office. Maybe we can get the latest police reports on Barry's death and your accident. It might clarify a few things." Ralph said.

I added. "The officer who visited me in the hospital was Lieutenant Hale. He seemed to have connected our crash with Barry's death. Hale warned me to stay out of it."

"I know that guy, Hale. He pretends to be a hard ass, but he can be reasonable. Let me make a few phone calls."

I watched Ralph as he dialed the number of his contact at the District Attorney's office. I listened to one side of Ralph's conversation, inserting my own words into the part of the other party.

"Nancy, this is Ralph Dowden. How are you? Yes, I miss her every day. I need a favor. You know I will. The untimely death of candidate Barry McGleam, the guy who was going to be your future boss. I need the list of suspects and the interviewed individuals. Great, send it to my fax line. You know I will. See you soon."

Then Ralph hung up.

"Whatever information the District Attorney has will be here shortly. I suspect your friend Hale may be holding back some information," he said.

"Hale is not my friend. And really? A fax? Why not email?"

"She can clear the memory on the fax machine, and no one will trace the call. Since faxes use an encrypted protocol, no one will know what information is being transmitted. "It's the safest way to send us the data," he said, emphasizing the lack of tracking.

I had just learned another of the secrets Ralph had in his P.I. toolbox. Ten years after I met him, I was still learning from Ralph.

A few minutes later, the phone rang. I heard a click. Ralph's multi-function copier, printer fax machine started emitting a bevy of beeps and squeals as the two fax machines transmitted their data across a voice-grade telephone line. Seconds later, the contraption started spitting out page after page of printed documents. After the whirring and beeping ceased, Ralph collected approximately fifteen pages of information.

"Okay," he said. "Let's see what we got."

"Looks like they interviewed Tiffany Burns. She claimed to have an alibi. Ms. Burns claims she was dancing at the Peppermint Lounge the night of Barry's death. She was on stage from 7:00 p.m. until midnight. That eliminates her based on opportunity, at least until we can verify her statement."

Reading on, he found the name Wallace Bolton. "From what it says here, they grilled Bolton pretty good. Not only did they dig into his whereabouts, but they also verified his alibi with members of his staff. Bolton was at a campaign fundraiser. A dozen people saw him there."

"What if he hired someone?" I added.

"Possible, we'll keep an open mind," he said.

Ralph chuckled. "I see your name on this list as well. You can find Hale's visit to your hospital room documented on this list. It seems to imply you're not a suspect in McGleam's murder, but that you might be an accessory to his killer, Jessica McGleam. How do you feel about that?"

"Not much I can do. If we can clear Jessica, it will clear me as well."

"There is no mention of this Sarah Thomas you had on your list. Are you sure she is involved? The police aren't even looking at her, and I don't see an obvious motive," Ralph remarked.

"Call it a hunch, but Sarah Thomas is Bolton's campaign manager, his girlfriend, and she is Tiffany Burn's aunt. I can't believe it's all a coincidence. There is something more there. I have no idea what it is."

"Okay, where does that leave us?" Ralph asked.

"I am going to dig deeper into Sarah Thomas' past. You work on poking holes in the alibis of the other suspects," I said.

I picked up the phone. It was time to check in with Thelma Jenkins. "Thelma, look at the Jessica Sekelsky file. I want you to dig up everything you can on Sarah Thomas. I mean everything. We need to know her age, her weight, her phone number, and what she eats for breakfast. I don't know what I am looking for, I'll notice it when I see it. Call me if you have questions."

"Yes sir, Mr. Body. I am on it right now."

I looked across the desk at Ralph. A smug expression adorned his face.

"What?" I asked.

"I thought you said YOU were going to dig into Sarah Thomas?" Ralph asked.

"It's called delegating. You should try it sometime, Ralph. Thelma's good at research. We have other tasks to handle.

"Okay, so what do you want to do? What's the plan?" Ralph asked.

"When our accident happened, the police on the scene only viewed it as a car crash. They probably thought a drunk or distracted driver caused it. I don't think they did any thorough Crime Scene Investigation. Their goal was to get the road cleared and back open to traffic. They probably had a wrecker haul the car away to an impound lot."

I continued, "Was the car ever examined for evidence of tampering? Did they even consider it to be a crime scene?"

"Most likely, they focused on the occupants and the damage. Saving you and Jessica's lives was their number one priority," said Ralph.

"Do you think we can get into the impound lot and inspect the wreckage of Jessica's car? It might reveal some clues that the police missed," I asked.

"Let me make a call. I know a guy. He's an estimator for insurance companies. Smart guy. He has access to the police impound lot. Maybe he can get us in there?"

Once again, Ralph's connections came through. His friend Marty O'Brien, a freelancer who worked as a damage estimator for several big insurance companies, agreed to meet us at 4:00 pm at the police impound lot near the Norfolk County jail in Dedham, just a few miles from Ralph's Natick home.

I remember one thing that Ralph taught me years ago. "People like to talk. Get them talking and your investigation will come together quickly."

Ralph and I spent the morning discussing the key players, but we agreed there might be others who observed the action. I was looking for anyone else with knowledge about what occurred on Tuesday night. That list might include friends, neighbors, and co-workers. Creating that list meant the day ahead promised to be a busy one.

While heading to the impound lot, I asked Ralph to make an unscheduled stop along the way at the Peppermint Lounge. The nightclub where Tiffany Burns worked nights. I wanted to check out the place. I knew it would be too early for the regular crowd. Still, we might learn something. Ralph was equally inquisitive, so we headed east, stopping first in Needham, MA. and the Peppermint Lounge.

✳ ✳ ✳

The Peppermint Lounge lived up to its reputation as a high-end gentlemen's club. A large modern building with lots of parking and tastefully designed signage that belied the seedy nature of its business.

Patrons enter through a lobby area where a cashier collects a cover charge and issues a ticket to the show. The lobby doubles as a greeting room where bouncers screen customers before entering the showroom. A sign on the wall advised customers, "No photography or video equipment allowed in the showroom." A second smaller sign warned, "No firearms in the performance area."

Stepping inside the showroom, we sensed the essence of a Las Vegas casino, a far cry from Big Benny's Kandy Shop. It sported clean, polished concrete floors and walls adorned with acoustic

150

sound-deadening panels of beige and brown. Straight ahead, I could see a big stage. There were ceiling-mounted spotlights, a sound system that could blast your ears off, and an enormous video screen behind the stage. The floor plan ensured everyone seated at the tables got a good view of the dancers by arranging the tables and chairs in a semi-circular fashion around the stage. Behind the bar were four television screens that replicated the onstage show for drinkers who preferred to belly up to the bar.

It was still early, and as suspected, the lounge was closed. Two Hispanic men were cleaning the floor and resetting the furniture. Behind the bar, a muscular young man with dark hair, a beard, and tattoos covering the length of both of his arms, was inventorying the booze, and restocking the shelves. I approached the bar, trying not to startle him.

I interrupted him, then thinking quickly, I made up a story to cover our presence. "Excuse me. We are investigating a missing truck that the owner says someone stole from your lot on Tuesday night. You know anything about it?"

"Who are you guys? Cops?" he asked.

"No, the police aren't helping. The truck owner hired us to investigate it on his behalf.

He shook his head. "Sorry, I can't help. No one said anything to me about it."

"The owner of the truck said he was drinking with a dancer named Tiffany. He thinks Tiffany might have lifted his keys from his pocket. Do you know a dancer named Tiffany?"

"Yeah, I know Tiffany. You guys are off base. Tiffany wouldn't do that. Besides, she doesn't need a pickup truck. Tiffany drives a

Porsche and lives in a penthouse condo in Wellesley. She's one of the most popular dancers in the club and the richest. Besides, I would believe her before I would believe some drunk who lost his truck."

Ralph asked. "I noticed you have cameras in the lot. Got any surveillance footage from Tuesday evening?"

"You'll have to talk to the boss. He won't be here until about five o'clock. Leave your name. He'll call you."

I pressed the issue. "Come on, you're not going to make us come back, are you? What's it going to take to get a copy now?"

"Sorry, the office is closed," he said.

I pulled a fifty-dollar bill out of my wallet. "Come on, give us a break. We're in a hurry. Do you think you might be able to scare up a copy? For President Grant?"

"I don't know. I have a ton of work here," he said. "Maybe Mr. Franklin might help make my job go quicker."

I reached back into my wallet and pulled out a one-hundred-dollar bill. I held it up so the barman could see the image of Benjamin Franklin.

One hundred dollars was too much for him to pass up. "What day did you say?" he asked.

"Tuesday, between 7:00 pm and midnight.

"Give me a couple of minutes. I'll see what I can find."

While we waited, we snooped around the room for clues. A whiteboard hung on the dressing room door. It looked like the evening schedule, with the names of the dancers and their performance times; Barbie – 8:05, Lexi – 8:15, Kandi – 8:25, and so on. I snapped a picture with my phone, hoping it might tell us something.

It took about fifteen minutes for the barman to return carrying a VHS videotape. "I made a copy of Tuesday's tape. I don't know what's on it. I didn't look."

I couldn't believe it, in this day and age. "A videotape? Seriously, that's the best you can do?"

"Hey, that's what we got. You want it or not?" he said.

Ralph looked at me and nodded. "I have a machine."

I handed the barman the crisp one-hundred-dollar bill. He handed me the tape.

"Good luck. We haven't had any disturbances here in weeks," he said.

As we left the Peppermint Lounge, I commented to Ralph. "That was probably the most expensive videotape I've ever bought. I hope there is something on it worth watching."

Ralph laughed, "That's why he said good luck. I hope you didn't waste your money."

Ralph jumped back into the driver's seat. "Let's head over to the impound. My buddy O'Brien should be there soon."

We arrived at the impound lot a few minutes early, but Ralph's buddy was already there waiting. Ralph introduced us, "Marty O'Brien, meet Able Body. He's a private investigator from Illinois. He was behind the wheel of the car we wish to examine."

Marty shuttled Ralph to the back of the lot. He knew that was the area where they brought the newly delivered wrecks. I hobbled behind on my crutches until we came upon Jessica's AMG, or what remained of it.

Seeing the wreckage brought me back to the crash night. I could still smell the burning rubber. I saw the mix of oil and antifreeze puddling along the roadside. The feeling of horror returned as I remembered crawling from the wreckage only to lie helpless on the cold, damp ground, waiting for someone to save me.

The accident obliterated the entire front of the car. Like a discarded sheet of paper, the crumpled remains of the hood lay to the side. The impact pulverized all the glass except the rear window. Several of the airbags in the cockpit deployed in the crash. Those airbags probably saved Jessica's and my lives. The area we occupied, the center console, the front seats and part of the dashboard were broken and askew.

At first glance, the rear of the car appeared undamaged, except for a small hole in the rear fender. Someone, probably the police, forced open the trunk and removed its contents. Most likely, they were searching for contraband or drugs.

I stood there frozen, staring at the wreckage until Marty commented, "Wow, nice car. This baby cost a pretty penny. Such a waste." He was right, such a waste.

We took turns poking around outside the remains of the wreckage, looking for clues. Unsure what to look for, we hoped to discover something unexpected. That's when Marty noticed something strange. Pulling down the trunk lid, he pointed to what looked like two round impact holes in the flat part of the panel an inch below the rear spoiler.

"Look here, and here," he said. Feeling one hole with his thumb. "These look like bullet holes."

Then a vision came into my head. I recalled hearing thumps like something was hitting the car. It didn't occur to me that the other car's driver could be shooting at us. If bullets aimed at us caused those holes, it could help prove our innocence. The police investigators may have missed an important clue.

Marty, an experienced insurance estimator, knew what clues to look for. He took a laser pen out of his pocket and stuck it in the hole in the center of the trunk lid. The beam shot through the trunk and penetrated between the rear seats into the car's interior.

He climbed onto what remained of the driver's front seat and, following the laser beam, he ran his hands across the dashboard, looking for more signs of damage. Subtle clues like this are easy to miss. Marty had to get down on his knees, below the line of sight. It was hard to see. At the bottom of the dashboard, a few inches from where the laser was pointing, Marty spotted a hole in the panel just above the accelerator pedal.

Marty pointed to the hole. "Look, the bullet came through this spot."

If it was a bullet hole, that could explain a lot. We needed to convince Hale a thorough examination of the car was in order. If a stray bullet damaged an important piece of electronics like the accelerator pedal or the computer that controls the electronic systems of the engine, that may have been the reason for the sudden acceleration I experienced. I remember telling Hale at the hospital that I was an excellent driver. This discovery may prove it wasn't me. It was a mechanical failure that caused the crash.

By finding the bullet, ballistics tests could help the police trace the gun. Then, ultimately, to the party that was chasing us. Those bullet holes were proof that someone wanted Jessica dead.

Convincing the police to re-examine Jessica's car was crucial. I thought calling Jessica's lawyer would be a smart approach. Hoping he could request further tests. Marty concurred that something wasn't right. He had a better idea. Marty owed Ralph a few favors, and he knew the police chief, Hale's boss. He agreed to alert the chief of his findings. Implying he might be called to be an expert witness in any upcoming trial, O'Brien could disrupt the outcome of the proceedings.

"They hate when outside witnesses muddy up their trials," he said.

A deeper investigation would most certainly anger Hale. His nice, neat case of a domestic squabble was about to get more complicated.

We left the impound lot with renewed optimism. Ralph's connections as a past insurance investigator were paying dividends.

In just one day we accomplished a lot. I got the videotape from the Peppermint Lounge, and Ralph got Marty to request a deeper investigation into the car crash. Without Ralph's help, my investigation would still be at square one.

In the car on our way home, Ralph broached a subject that was on both our minds.

"Able, I'm sorry, but I gotta ask. Who's paying for all of this? I mean, I am on board with the gas and the food and miscellaneous expenses. But you just dropped a hundred bucks getting that video.

Before this investigation ends, we'll probably bribe several other people. Where is the money coming from?"

I didn't have an honest answer, so I made one up. "Jessica McGleam stands to inherit a fortune from the estate of her late husband. When she recovers, I'll send her an itemized bill."

"You mean if she recovers," he said.

Ralph had a point. Although she was no longer dependent on the ventilator, Jessica still had a long journey ahead. She needed several more surgeries and months of physical therapy. There was always the risk of complications.

"If she doesn't, I guess I'll be applying for government assistance. Know anybody who will hire a broke private detective?"

Ralph didn't reply. He just stared straight ahead.

Whichever way you look at it, the futures of Able Body and Jessica Sekelsky-McGleam looked cloudy at best.

We drove on for several minutes in silence. Then Ralph turned toward me. "I am sorry this happened to you, kid.

I understand how it feels to be in love with a woman. My wife and I were in love for thirty-six years. I still love her. I would have given everything I owned to save her. I couldn't."

We headed back towards Ralph's home in Natick with little more to say. Despite their differences, the two partners discovered they shared many interests. I kept thinking about each suspect and each of their alibis. I had a hunch there was something we weren't seeing. But what?

Then, as if on cue, my phone rang. It was Thelma Jenkins reporting back with the information she discovered about Sarah Thomas.

"I am putting you on speakerphone so my partner Ralph can hear as well," I said.

A few seconds later, I gave her the okay. "Okay Thelma, what have you got?"

"Oh boy, I have a lot to tell you," she said.

"The night of the murder, Wallace Bolton was holding a fundraiser at his campaign headquarters. A crowd of people attended. Fifty people, maybe more. They posted pictures of the event all over social media. Bolton posed for pictures with supporters holding up checks to show his campaign was successful at raising money. The time stamps on the pictures prove that he was at the fundraiser from before 7:00 p.m. until after 10:00 p.m. He has a solid alibi.

"Here's the kicker, though. The lady you told me to check out only appears in shots in the beginning at about 7:00 p.m. She disappears from the pictures but reappears again at about 9:55 p.m. just before the event ends. When did you mention being followed?"

I remembered driving past Bolton's headquarters about 8:30 p.m. That is when the reporter spotted us. Seconds later, the blue SUV started following us.

"Wait, there's more," she said. "In the first couple of pictures, there's a young man with Sarah Thomas. A big guy, with a dark beard, about thirty years old. Just like Sarah, he disappears from the pictures and reappears later. The social media posts identified him as Jason Callahan."

"So, both Thomas and Callahan have an unexplained disappearance from the event?" I asked.

"Yes, so. I kept digging. Jason Callahan, it turns out, is Sarah Thomas' son from a previous marriage."

"Hmm," interjects Ralph. "The plot thickens."

"Wait," said Thelma. "You haven't heard the best part. Jason Callahan's father, Larry Callahan, ran a protection racket in South Boston for the mob. He died in prison four years ago. Guess who helped put him in jail?"

"Wait," said Able. "Don't tell me. Barry McGleam?"

"Right on," said Thelma. "Sarah Thomas and Jason Callahan had a huge revenge motive to kill Barry McGleam. Even better, if they could pin it on Jessica, they would be home free. Sarah Thomas may even have been using Tiffany Burns as a smokescreen to set up Barry. Tiffany may have lured him to his campaign headquarters the night of the murder."

"Thelma, I could kiss you. Send me everything you discovered. I must convince the police to review this evidence.

"Oh, Mr. Body. You are making me blush."

Hearing the details of Thelma's research, I knew where I wanted to go next. I wanted to get a close-up look at Sarah Thomas and Jason Callahan.

"Ralph," I asked. "Would you mind taking a detour? I want to check out Bolton's campaign headquarters."

"I don't mind at all. It's time to talk to Sarah Thomas. Let's go," replied Ralph.

Ralph turned the car east, heading toward Needham. Taking a slight detour to Bolton's offices could lead us to better answers.

We posed as voters who had questions about Bolton's stand on a variety of hot-button issues a District Attorney candidate might support or sponsor.

Before we went inside, Ralph made detailed notes of the parking lot and which cars were parked there. He snapped a few pictures, ensuring clear views of the license plates. He also surveyed the exterior of the building, noticing the presence of security cameras near the front door and the rear of the building.

Stepping inside, we found the walls plastered with signs and slogans touting Bolton's ability to fix every problem the world faces today. Many of the posters had Bolton's smiling face urging the reader to vote for Bolton. One sign claimed Bolton was *The Cure For What Ails Us*.

Rows of desks lined both sides of an aisle, with offices along the west wall. On one desk near the front door was a tip jar where someone could make an anonymous cash donation. The jar only contained a few dollars.

The room was quiet except for one person, working in the office, a woman we recognized to be Sarah Thomas. Ralph waved his hand to call her over.

I had my phone in my hand. At first, Ralph thought I was being rude, but quickly realized I was videotaping the offices.

I whispered to Ralph. "Distract her for a few minutes. I want to look at something."

Scanning the building, I noticed an equipment room at the rear of the offices. I spotted a printer, a large copier, and what appeared to be an internet router inside. I needed to get back there.

Thinking quickly, I asked Sarah if I could use the restroom. She gestured towards the building's rear. I winked at Ralph and then headed toward the back room.

Ralph knew I was up to something. But what? He did his best to distract Sarah Thomas, keeping her eyes focused on him or Bolton's campaign propaganda. He asked her pointed questions about Bolton's stand on crime. She replied with practiced answers.

Sarah handed Ralph their latest campaign literature. She fed him the standard lines detailing Bolton's political agenda and how he would make life better for Norfolk County residents. Then, with all the poise of a used car salesperson, she encouraged him to donate to Bolton's campaign.

As soon as I returned, Sarah gave me the same sales pitch she gave Ralph. I smiled and nodded in agreement. We took the campaign materials and thanked Sarah, promising to support Bolton on Election Day.

Just as Ralph and I were ending our conversation with Thomas, Jason Callahan walked in the door. Ralph approached Jason and shook his hand. A big strong young man, he seemed to be out of breath. Ralph, with his dry sense of humor, kidded Jason, claiming he must have been out strong-arming some last-minute voters. Maybe it was the generation gap, but Jason didn't get the joke.

We continued on our way, bidding Sarah and Jason good luck. Once we were alone outside the building, Ralph inquired, "What were you doing in there?"

"I used the trick you showed me with the WPS button on the internet router to connect my phone to the Wi-Fi. I think we might hack their network, maybe even crack into their computers. Let's plan to come back later after they close. Maybe we can download their emails and review their calendars."

My cunning action had Ralph beaming with pride. "See, you thought I was past my prime. I taught you something you can use in your investigations."

"Ralph," I replied. "I never thought of you that way. You're a talented investigator and an excellent teacher."

While returning to Ralph's car, I spotted a new car in the lot. The blue SUV bore a striking resemblance to the car that had caused our accident. I walked over and using my bare hand touched the hood. It was still warm. The heat suggested the engine had just been running. It was likely Jason Callahan's car. I bent over to inspect the bumper. I saw no visible damage, but I did spot white paint flecks on the left side. Jessica's car was white. It could be the paint from her AMG.

I knew immediately it was Callahan who ran us off the road. Angered, I declared. "I'm calling the police; this is the car."

Ralph tempered me. "Wait, we need more proof. Take some pictures of the car. We can come back later and see if we can crack their network. Maybe we can get more information. Then we can go to Hale."

I took pictures of the SUV including the license number and close-ups of the paint on the bumper. Our visit to Bolton's office catapulted Sarah Thomas and Jason Callahan to the top of our list of prime suspects. Now we just needed to prove our theory.

By the time we returned to Ralph's house, it was getting late. I champed at the bit to get busy viewing the videotape from the Peppermint Lounge. I could tell Ralph was tired. He wanted to make dinner and wind down the day's activities. We compromised by ordering a pizza and rehashing the events of the day.

After chowing down on a thin crust, pepperoni and sausage pizza and a small glass of chianti wine poured from a jug, Ralph retired to the couch. Just before dark, he closed his eyes. A few short minutes later, he was snoring like a chainsaw.

When we were at Bolton's office, I tapped into the Wi-Fi network. I still hoped to make it back to the campaign office to hack their network. Without a rental car, I had to shelve that operation for another day. Still, we accomplished a lot with our visits to The Peppermint Lounge, the impound lot, and Bolton's headquarters. It was time to call it a day and resume our work tomorrow.

THE PORSCHE AND THE PRIVATE DANCER

I was ready to implicate Jason Callahan in our car crash, but Ralph tempered my fervor. He wanted to keep the murder investigation going. He wanted more evidence. Viewing the videotape from the Peppermint Lounge was still his focus.

Ralph went down to his basement and returned with an ancient VHS tape player and a pair of old-fashioned audio and video cables that we could use to connect to my computer.

"You can't get these things anymore," he said. "I kept it in storage, just in case. Even old equipment comes in handy."

He dusted the unit off and then connected it to my laptop.

"I haven't used it in years. Let's test it to make sure it is in good working condition before we insert your one-hundred-dollar tape." He inserted a specially designed head cleaning tape into the front slot and the black box whirred to life. The old unit functioned as expected working through a cleaning and testing routine that confirmed its operation. Ralph's antiquated machine was once again a valuable asset. He smiled knowingly.

I pulled his test tape from the machine and slid the tape I bought from the bartender into the slot. In seconds, a picture appeared on the screen. The video showed footage from the camera mounted on the roof of the building. It panned back and forth across the parking lot. Watching a videotape of the cars in a parking lot is only slightly more entertaining than watching paint dry. At first, the lot was empty. Around 6:55 p.m. the activity started.

One by one, the young female dancers arrived, pulling their cars into parking spaces near the rear door. The video quality sufficed enough to discern the identities of the people. We could identify the car models and their license plate numbers.

I watched as Tiffany Burns pulled her hot pink Porsche 911 with the license plate PVTDNCR into the front row near the back of the building. She climbed out and strolled calmly toward the back door, out of camera range.

Minutes later, the lot started filling up with Mercedes convertibles, Lexus sedans, and a mix of exotic sports cars and luxury SUVs. Men of all ages, dressed in blue and gray business suits, adorned with fancy ties, filtered in through the front door.

It seemed like a normal evening at the Peppermint Lounge. Until the 7:22 p.m. time stamp. That's when I spotted a woman who resembled Tiffany Burns get in her car and drive away. It seemed Tiffany lied to the police, by providing an alibi that she was on stage during Barry's shooting.

We continued to watch other cars come and go, but none of the other dancers left the building. She returned twenty-five minutes later, just in time for her next dance performance. The video proved that Tiffany could have left the Peppermint Lounge, killed Barry, and returned to work in time to support her alibi.

Tiffany's means, motive, and opportunity placed her back in the category of primary suspect. To me, this entire investigation was becoming confusing. Was it Tiffany? Sarah? Jason? Any or all of them could have committed Barry's murder. My head started throbbing. We needed more help. Help from someone with enough authority and resources to investigate deeper. We only knew one person, Lieutenant Hale. Hale was the guy we needed to get more involved in the mystery.

I was just about to pick up the phone and call Lieutenant Hale's office when Ralph's doorbell rang. A second later, someone pounded violently on the door. Ralph looked through the peephole to see an impatient Lieutenant Hale rocking nervously on his porch.

"Well, well. It's Hale," Ralph called out as he opened the door.

Hale barged in, screaming. "Where's that asshole Body?"

Hale bounced back and forth, attempting to look past Ralph, trying to locate me, as if I were hiding. I wasn't hiding. Hearing the ruckus, I limped to the vestibule where the other two men stood.

"Lieutenant Hale," I said, "How can I help you?"

An angry Lieutenant Hale snapped. Pointing his finger over Ralph's shoulder, he screamed at me, "I warned you to stay out of my investigation. Your license is in Illinois. I ought to lock you up right now for obstruction of justice."

"I am a licensed Private Investigator," Ralph interjected. "Mr. Body is working for me as a research assistant."

"Perfect," chided Hale. "An old has-been gumshoe from Natick and his sidekick, the Undercover Brother from Smallville, Illinois. The dynamic duo."

Ralph remained calm after Hale's insult. Then he stopped Hale's tirade in its tracks.

"If you were doing your job, we wouldn't be involved. Do you want me to call your captain now and complain about you busting in here? Or do you prefer I call the media and let them decide if you are doing your job?"

Hale was stuck. He could talk his way out of busting into Dowden's residence, but the last thing he needed was bad press. His captain doesn't take kindly to putting the Norfolk County police under the microscope.

Ralph, in a calm clear voice, continued, "Perhaps you should listen to what this old gumshoe and his partner have found in their investigation?"

Hale was no dummy. He knew his investigation existed mostly of circumstantial evidence. He reluctantly nodded his head in agreement.

"Come this way, Officer," said Ralph.

"It's Lieutenant," said Hale. "Address me as Lieutenant, I have at least earned that much respect."

"Lieutenant," Ralph repeated.

Ralph offered Hale a chair across from our desks. "I think you will be interested in hearing what we have discovered," he said.

I started. "As you know, I believe the crash Jessica and I were involved in last week wasn't an accident. It was part of a bigger scheme that included the death of Barry McGleam. Our investigation into people of interest has uncovered inconsistencies in their alibis. Tiffany Burns claimed to be at work at the time of Barry's death. But I found videotape evidence that shows her leaving the Peppermint Lounge and returning during that same period when Barry was killed."

I queued up the video that showed Tiffany getting into her car at 7:22 p.m. Pointing to the screen, I said, "I think we need to find out where she went and what she did."

"That proves nothing," said Hale.

"No, it doesn't, but it proves she had the opportunity. We already know she had a motive. Since your people never found a murder weapon, we cannot prove anything yet. But I would suggest you re-interview Ms. Burns. She isn't telling you the complete story about what happened that night."

Taking a deep breath, Hale let out a long sigh. He didn't say it, but our discovery swayed Hale's thinking. Perhaps he realized there's more to this story than he thought. Suddenly, Hale's cut-and-dried case against Jessica wasn't so clear. He had more work to do. Thanks to the has-been sleuth and the Undercover Brother from Smallville.

While jotting down a note in his pocket-sized notepad, Hale commented. "I don't know how you got this video. If you haven't acquired it legally, we won't be able to use it."

"The bartender gave it to us voluntarily," I assured Hale.

"Still, I'll request a warrant to secure a copy from the owner of the Peppermint Lounge. I will start working on it immediately."

He expressed his frustration. "The current District Attorney, Tommy Boyle, has been hounding me to charge someone with murder. He doesn't like the idea that his heir apparent has met an untimely death. It's screwing up the election, and it looks bad for him and the D.A.'s office. I have been stalling him until Jessica regains consciousness. I'm not sure how much longer I can stall."

"If you charge Jessica too soon, it's going to blow up in your face. You better bring Tiffany in for more questioning," said Ralph.

"She will lawyer up for sure. If she isn't the killer, we might tip our hand too soon. What else you got?" Hale asked.

Ralph took this one. "We also are looking into Sarah Thomas, Bolton's campaign manager. We made some discoveries that may implicate her as a person of interest."

"Sarah Thomas? That's ridiculous. Why would she want McGleam dead?" asked Hale.

"We may have discovered some evidence that Ms. Thomas and her son had a grudge against McGleam. Barry was a member of the team that prosecuted Thomas' husband, Larry Callahan, six years ago. It was that high-profile trial that got Barry noticed by the party. Despite Callahan being a small-time crook, McGleam bragged often about how he helped put a big-time mobster in jail. It sorta became his hallmark case as a law-and-order guy."

Ralph continued. "Larry Callahan died in prison. There was no love lost between Sarah Thomas and Barry McGleam. Sarah's son Jason is twenty-eight now. He has a reputation for causing trouble. He might be responsible for this entire mess."

Hale paused for a second, rethinking the evidence. "Or Sarah Thomas could be the brains and Jason the enforcer. But I can't just go accusing them without evidence."

I chimed in. "We have more. Jason Callahan drives a blue SUV. It looks a lot like the car that followed us Tuesday night. I checked it out. He has a little white paint on his bumper from another car. It could be a match for the paint on Jessica's AMG. If the paint matches, we can tie Jason to the crash. You need to get a warrant to search and inspect Jason's SUV."

"Holy shit," replied Hale. "You guys have been busy."

That is when Ralph again surprised me with his perspicacity. "I understand that in your experience, the disgruntled spouse is always the chief suspect, but you were taking the easy way out. You need to take action now to ensure the evidence doesn't vanish."

Hale sat silently, contemplating what Ralph had just said. His stance softened. "I hope you guys are wrong. We will look into your allegations. I want to do what is right."

"Have you gotten any evidence back from Jessica's car? We need to find that bullet."

Hale didn't know it was us who contacted his chief to request a reexamination of Jessica's car. He thought it was the insurance company. He had been keeping his cards close to his chest. Not telling anyone what they found.

Before today's revelations, Hale still clung to the belief that the car crash was an unrelated road rage incident.

Hale sighed again. "I probably shouldn't be telling you this. The CSI investigators discovered a bullet lodged beneath the car's dashboard. They think it may have damaged the cruise control module. That would explain your claim of the sudden acceleration that caused your crash.

"The forensic team is running ballistics tests as we speak. We won't know until tomorrow if the bullet in the dash matches the bullets that killed McGleam."

Still trying to defend his original theory, he said, "If they don't match, we will prove the two incidents are not related."

"But if they do?" I challenged.

"Then all bets are off. We will find out what happened."

I looked at Ralph. Ralph looked back at me. I knew what Ralph was thinking. The evidence we found was surprisingly impressive for a small-town hack and past-his-prime gumshoe.

"Lieutenant," I said. "They need to be questioned again. All of them. Ralph and I want to be present as observers. I think considering all the information we just shared with you, we have earned that right."

Hale didn't like the idea of two private detectives hijacking his investigation. He pondered his next course of action. Lieutenant Hale looked around the room. He started offering a mild protest, then paused again. After a few seconds, he conceded.

Looking directly at Ralph he said, "I will communicate with you, Mr. Dowden. Everything needs to be above board."

Then, turning toward me, he said, "Body, let me remind you, that your association with Jessica McGleam still makes you a person of interest. If we find out your traffic accident resulted from illegal activity, the County Sheriff may cite you for traffic violations. I would tread lightly if I were you."

"Our goal is to see justice done, no matter who it affects," I said.

Hale jumped up from his seat. He looked at his watch, noting the time. "Gentlemen, I will leave you now. My workload is overwhelming. The next few days will be filled with activity."

Hale left Ralph's house with a long list of tasks he needed to complete. As soon as he was out of sight, I turned to Ralph. Anxious to get out on my own, I said, "Ralph, I appreciate the help you have given me, but it is time for me to get a rental car."

"Do you think you should be driving with your foot still in that cast?"

"Yes, I am ready. Besides, it's my left foot. I can drive an automatic transmission with only my right. If you don't mind, run me over to the nearest rental car agency. I'd like to spend some extra time at the hospital visiting Jessica.

Ralph walked into the kitchen and rummaged around in a drawer near the refrigerator. He turned toward me. "Here's a house key. You can come and go as necessary."

I got online and found a car rental agency right in Natick that had a nondescript white economy sedan at an affordable rate. I reserved the car for three days. Hopefully, in three days, we can wrap up the investigation and I can make plans to return home to Berwyn.

Thirty minutes later, the odd couple was seated in Ralph's SUV, pulling up in front of a rental car office in downtown Natick.

"Will you be home in time for dinner?" asked Ralph.

It made me laugh. "You sound like my father. I plan to have a sit-down conversation with Jessica's parents, the Sekelskys. There are matters we need to discuss. I'll be home late. Go ahead and eat without me."

"Okay, I'll review the evidence to ensure we haven't overlooked anything. If Hale contacts me, I'll let you know." Ralph reached out to shake my hand. "Good luck, young man."

Ralph Dowden exceeded all expectations as my partner. Despite not working together for ten years, he was still teaching me both detective skills and life skills. Ralph's help was paramount in this investigation. Now, it was my turn to take action. I needed some time alone to think.

When I was lying in the hospital bed, I promised myself I would break whatever spell Jessica Sekelsky had over me. My whole life, since our days in high school, has been with me, trying to make Jessica happy. It was her lying unconscious in a hospital bed. I knew it wasn't the time for me to walk away. Yet, I knew if she recovered. If she could be the same Jessica Sekelsky-McGleam she was before the accident. There's a chance our relationship could begin again.

I loved Jessica. I loved Mr. and Mrs. Sekelsky. No parent should have to endure watching their child lying in a hospital bed, broken, suffering, or maybe dying. I could only offer them moral support if she didn't recover. If she recuperates, I must bid them a fond farewell. If Ralph Dowden taught me nothing else, he showed me that Able Body must take control of his own life.

When I arrived at the hospital, I found the Sekelskys, ever-present, at Jessica's side.

I thought. "They must be exhausted."

Mr. Sekelsky looked like death warmed over. Trying to hold his emotions inside, trying to be strong, was taking its toll on the old man. I worried about who would die first, Jessica, or her father.

Marian Sekelsky smiled when she saw me peeking into the window of Jessica's hospital room. Disregarding the hospital's "Family Only" policy, she promptly opened the door.

"Please come in, Able. We are just sitting here talking with Jess."

George got up from his chair. "Here, sit here, Able," he offered.

"She just came back from another surgery. They repaired the muscle in her leg." With cautious optimism in her voice, she said. "Her condition is improving."

I offered to stay with Jessica. "Listen, if you two need a break, I will stay with Jessica. It looks like you could use some sleep."

"We have been taking turns. I think we both could use a break," said Marian.

"Take as long as you need. I will stay with her until you come back," I replied.

I took a seat next to Jessica, hoping the ICU nurse would not kick me out. Even though the doctors kept Jessica heavily sedated, it helped her to have a loved one nearby. I looked at her, remembering how beautiful she was as a young woman. Now she was lying there wrapped in bandages, looking frail and vulnerable.

"Jess, it's Able. I am here," I whispered. "I won't leave you. Pretty soon you will be back home in Berwyn. There's no need to worry."

That was all I could do. Sit and wait. Wait for whatever was going to happen next. Wait for Lieutenant Hale and the Norfolk police to get their act together and sort out this whole mess. Thank God I had Ralph Dowden on my side. Thank God I had Thelma Jenkins helping us from Berwyn. I thanked God I survived the crash. If I hadn't, Hale would have charged Jessica, and the actual killer would have gone free.

I was sound asleep in the big brown leather upholstered chair the nursing staff brought in for Mr. Sekelsky, holding Jessica's hand, when the ICU nurse came into the room. She looked at me with concern. She knew I wasn't family, and she didn't want to get in trouble for violating hospital policy.

"Where are Mrs. McGleam's parents?"

"They were tired. They needed a break. I offered to stay with Jessica."

She winked at me. "I didn't know she had a brother."

"I'm estranged," I said. "I had a different father and a different mother."

The nurse looked at me, unsure whether to laugh or snap at me for violating the hospital rules.

"I've come across situations like that before," she stated.

The nurse reviewed Jessica's vital signs, checked her intravenous medicines, and assessed the condition of her bandages. Everything looked normal.

Before leaving the room, she stated, "I'll be back in an hour. If you need anything, use the call button. We are right outside."

She understood sometimes the closest family members are not blood relatives. I was alone again with Jessica and my thoughts.

The Sekelskys were gone for several hours. Although I was willing to give them a break, time was passing, and I had to rejoin Ralph and Hale to reignite the investigation into Barry's murder.

Finally, the Sekelskys returned to Jessica's ICU room. George looked much better. "We managed to eat and rest for a while. I showered as well. I feel better," he said.

Marian came over and hugged me, placing a kiss on my cheek. "Thank you, Able, for coming back to us. I am sure Jess knows you are here."

We sat together chatting about the old neighborhood and people we remembered from Berwyn. For the Sekelskys, Berwyn was the center of their world. Jessica's decision to move away from her childhood home displeased them.

A few minutes later, our conversation was interrupted by the doctor who performed Jessica's last surgery.

"How's our patient doing?" he asked.

Marian replied, "We are praying."

"Let's take a look," he said. He studied her chart, then examined the wound where he had repaired the muscle.

"She's strong," he said. "The swelling in her brain is gone. She's getting better every day. If we can avoid infection, I think we may be able to wean her off the sedatives. She'll need some physical therapy, but I am optimistic she'll recover quickly."

I watched George make the sign of the cross, and then bow his head in prayer. Marian rubbed his back reassuringly. His little girl was being tested. He needed god's help.

The doctor's positive comments buoyed their spirits. Jessica was getting better.

There was nothing more I could do. I looked at my phone. It was time to continue my hunt for the killer of Barry McGleam. I hoped I could find the killer before Jessica woke up. I wanted to be the one to break the news to her.

"Mr. and Mrs. Sekelsky," I said. "I have to go. I have someone I need to meet. Will you be alright here?"

"Yes, Able," Marian replied. "Thank you. We'll let you know if anything changes."

I hobbled on my crutches, my foot still encased in a fiberglass cast, down the hall, climbed into the elevator, and walked out the front door of the hospital. Once again, I grabbed my phone. This time, I called Ralph Dowden to see if Hale was providing any updates.

"Nothing yet," said Ralph. "How are things going at the hospital?"

"It's going well. The doctors are optimistic. We'll just have to wait and see. Call me if anything changes."

Before I left the hospital campus, I visited the physical therapist who earlier helped me get used to the crutches at his office near the main hospital building. He liked the progress I was making. After a little begging, he agreed to remove the cast and helped fit me with an orthopedic walking boot. I still had some pain, but I paced around the room showing him my dexterity. He smiled at my determination. "Okay," he said. "Looks like you are good to go. Just take it easy."

Without the crutches, my mobility improved. I was finally getting back to normal.

* * *

Starved, I opened an app on my phone to look for a good diner where I could get a steak and mashed potatoes or a grilled pork chop with applesauce. No reflection on Ralph, but if I had one more bowl of chili or a piece of fried chicken, I would puke. I found a restaurant that specialized in Greek cuisine called Cosmos.

The menu included grilled octopus, lamb chops, baklava, and other Greek-inspired dishes. No chili, thank God.

I climbed into my rental car and pulled out of the parking lot, heading east toward the town of Walpole. Even without GPS, I was becoming familiar with the roads and towns in Norfolk County. I could understand why people, including the McGleam family, loved living here. The area was green and lush. Small lakes and sloughs dotted the countryside, and the small towns maintained a feeling of history and bygone days.

I never made it to Cosmos for dinner. Before I even got a mile from the hospital, my phone dinged. Ralph texted me. "I just got a message from Hale. He's bringing Tiffany Burns in for questioning right now. Meet me at the Norfolk County Sheriff's station in Dedham. Tell the desk sergeant you are there for a lineup with Hale."

I pulled to the side of the road and stopped my car. Texting back, "I'm on my way." My focus shifted away from dinner and back to the investigation.

I found the location of the Norfolk County Sheriff's Office on my phone's maps app. It was in the opposite direction but according to the app I could be there in fifteen minutes. I hit the gas and then spun the steering wheel around until the car was heading toward Dedham and the first significant opportunity to piece together the events of the last ten days as they happened in real-time.

Talking to myself, I muttered, "Hold on Jess, I'm going to solve this mystery. One way or another."

When I arrived at the sheriff's office parking lot, the sun had already gone down. I walked through the front door and approached the desk sergeant.

I introduced myself as a witness who was there to meet with Lieutenant Hale. A uniformed police officer escorted me to the second floor, past an area of desks I assumed belonged to the small group of detectives under Hale's command. We walked down a narrow hall to a room with a long glass wall.

The room serves as a safe space for witnesses to identify suspects without fear or intimidation. For this interrogation, I saw Hale seated across a table from Tiffany Burns. Ralph had arrived a few minutes earlier and nodded to me. Hale had instructed him to be quiet, as the rooms weren't soundproof.

Hale started with the most basic question. "Where were you Tuesday at 7:30 p.m., the night of Barry McGleam's death?"

"I already told you I was working at the Peppermint Lounge all night."

"And you never left?"

Tiffany squirmed in her seat. "I ran to Starbucks for a Frappuccino, but I came back ten minutes later."

"Did you pay a visit to Barry McGleam's campaign headquarters?"

Unsure how to respond, she clammed up.

"Ms. Burns, I asked you a question."

Not wanting to lie again, she replied, "I want a lawyer."

"Yes, that is your right. I'll arrange for you to make a phone call. While you wait for them to arrive. I want you to think about your situation. If you are innocent, you would be wise to tell us what you know."

Hale got up. Leaving the room briefly, he returned with a wireless telephone. Not a cell phone, the kind of handset that works through a landline network. "Here's the phone. You got one call. Make it good. I will be back in five minutes."

Leaving Tiffany alone to make her call, Hale walked into the room where Ralph and I were watching. "You probably heard; she lawyered up. It'll take some time before we know if she has legal representation. You should know that before we brought her in, we secured a search warrant to examine her phone. One of my detectives is going through her call history. We should know more in a while."

I still hadn't eaten. "Where can I grab a bite to eat?" I asked.

"You might find leftover donuts in the coffee room down the hall. If you want more, there's a sandwich shop across the street."

Not being a police officer, I didn't share the passion for leftover donuts that Hale's team members might have. I opted for the sandwich shop. "Can I bring you guys anything?"

Both Hale and Dowden declined. Ralph asked Hale. "Point me towards your restroom."

I scurried across the street and ordered a turkey and cheese sandwich on a hard roll and a soft drink. I devoured the sandwich as if it were my final feast, then hurried back upstairs to the observation room. Thirty minutes later, a young attorney from a trendy law firm that advertises on television walked into the station. They immediately guided him to the interrogation room. He introduced himself to Tiffany Burns as Robert Semtack.

Looking at Lieutenant Hale, he said. "I need a minute to confer with my client."

Hale exited the room. A couple of minutes later, he returned, and in his hands, he had a computer printout of Tiffany Burns' phone call log. He also had snapshots his detective salvaged from the video files of Tiffany Burns leaving the Peppermint Lounge at 7:22 p.m.

He spread the papers across the table. Tiffany's face turned white as a ghost.

"Ms. Burns, I think you are lying. These papers contradict your two earlier statements. It's never good to lie to a police officer."

Semtack looked over the papers. Again, he instructed Hale. "I am going to need another minute to confer with my client."

Hale stood up. Before leaving the room, he cautioned Semtack, "This time, try to get it right."

Ralph and I watched as Tiffany and her lawyer discussed her situation and the evidence Hale had presented to them.

After about five minutes, Hale returned to the interrogation. He sat there staring at Tiffany, waiting. Like a ticking timer, Hale drummed his fingers on the table.

Tiffany caught Semtack's gaze before turning to Hale, declaring, "I want to make a statement."

"Keep in mind everything you say in this room is recorded," Hale reminded her.

Ralph and I listened as she recounted the events of that night.

"I was between shows. I go on for ten minutes every hour. I usually hang out in the dressing room when I'm not on stage. Sometimes I do private dances for the clients. Just after my first show, I got a call from my Aunt Sarah. She called me to let me know she had seen Barry with another girl earlier in the day. She said she saw them go to Barry's office. I went there to confront him.

"I realize now that Sarah only called to rile me up. I knew Barry cheated on his wife with me, but he promised me as soon as the election was over, he was going to divorce her. If he was dating another woman, that meant he lied to me as well. I was tired of being strung along.

"I went to his office to stand up to him. He needed to shit or get off the pot. When I arrived, the door was open. Barry was already dead on the floor, surrounded by a pool of blood. I only stepped inside for a second, there was no one else inside. I didn't touch anything. I knew it was a setup, so I high-tailed it out of there."

Hale asked, "Why didn't you call the police?"

"I was scared. You would have arrested me on the spot. I felt stupid, like the jilted lover."

"What if he was still alive? You could have saved his life."

She shook her head. "I've seen dead bodies before. He was dead."

She paused for a second, then looked straight at Hale. "I didn't kill Barry McGleam. I had no motive. Alive Barry bought me gifts, he took me on vacations, and he gave me money. He's no good to me dead."

"Maybe you were angry? A crime of passion?"

"There's no maybe about it. I was angry. But not angry enough to kill him. Besides, I don't even have access to a gun. No motive, no means," she said.

Hale became aggressive. "Based on what you just told me, I can charge you with murder right now, Ms. Burns."

Semtack piped in, "You have no proof. You will never get these charges to stick, so stop intimidating my client. You're wasting time grilling her while the real killer is getting away.

"If there is nothing more, Lieutenant Hale, my client has been here for hours. If she's not being charged, we'd like to leave now."

Hale knew his case was flimsy at best. He needed more evidence to prove Tiffany Burns was the killer.

"We are not done here, Ms. Burns. I would advise you to stay in town and stay out of trouble. We will be talking again."

Tiffany Burns and her lawyer, Robert Semtack, got up and left the room. Hale sat there steaming. His nice, cut-and-dry investigation had turned into a mess. He was stuck, mired in the cesspool of society. Cheating husbands, exotic dancers, political opponents, dead mobsters, and private investigators from another city, all with their noses in his business.

After a minute, Hale got up. I hadn't noticed, but today he looked tired. His eyes looked tired, and his shoulders slumped. Walking into the room, where Ralph and I were still hanging out, he declared.

"Gentlemen, I am calling it a day. I have been working sixteen hours a day since this thing started. Yesterday I called my son by the wrong name. I need some sleep. We will pick this up tomorrow. Mr. Dowden, I will message you if I have something to share."

Ralph and I left the police station. "Ralph, I will see you at home. Before I return to Natick, I need to check on something." I didn't tell him where I was going. I knew he might disagree with my idea.

I hopped into my rental car and headed toward Needham and the campaign offices of Wallace Bolton. It was there I hoped to get one more look at Jason Callahan's blue SUV. Passing through the upscale side of town, to the poorer side, Bolton's offices were locked up tight, and the parking lot was empty. The streets lay deserted, and all the businesses closed. Except for the streetlights and a single neon sign in the window of a small restaurant named China Joy, about one hundred feet to the west of Bolton's offices, which still glowed "Open", it was dark and eerie.

I was the only one there, with no passersby and only an occasional car cruising past. I could understand everything being closed up at 9:00 p.m. if this were Berwyn, but in Needham, it was still early.

With no one around, this was the perfect time for me to try my hand at accessing Bolton's Wi-Fi network.

When I worked at M.I.A. and More, one of the experienced P.I.s taught me to always survey the situation for hidden trouble and, above all, remain invisible. I cruised the streets to confirm my observations were correct.

Needing a reason to be parked near Bolton's headquarters, I decided to use the restaurant as a cover. It was close enough to access the Wi-Fi signal and not be suspicious. I found a parking spot about fifty feet past Bolton's front door, about halfway between the two buildings.

Climbing out of the car and hobbling in my walking boot, I stepped inside the restaurant. They were cleaning up, but still had a couple of servings of chicken-fried rice in the wok. I bought one order, taking the container, some chopsticks, and a cup of water to drink. It was a perfect stratagem. If anyone questioned why I was there, it was simple: I was eating my carry-out food.

With my gambit in place, I accessed my phone's network settings to locate Bolton's Wi-Fi network. I found one labeled "WB_CampHQ". Selecting that network, I hoped my phone would remember the access code from the day before. It did, and an instant later, the little symbol displaying radio waves appeared in the upper corner of my screen. I established my network connection. When they closed for the day, Bolton's staff left the router and server running. My foot was in the door, virtually.

Without my laptop, the amount of data I could collect on my phone was limited. Fortunately, I had an adapter cable that connected my phone to a thumb drive. Rather than try hacking the network, I used a File Transfer Protocol program to perform a bulk download of all of Bolton's email, calendar data, and meeting minutes. There wasn't time to view the data. Instead, I would wait until I returned to Ralph's to analyze the files using my laptop.

The file transfer was just finishing up when a Needham patrol car cruised past. He slowed long enough to check me out. When he saw me trying to scoop fried rice into my mouth from a cardboard box, using chopsticks, he drove on past. My ruse worked. I completed the file transfer and dropped the Wi-Fi connection.

I still hadn't gotten what I came for. That was to examine Callahan's SUV more closely. Using an app on my phone that provides telephone numbers and addresses, I looked up the name Jason Callahan. I found one entry not too far away in Needham Heights. It couldn't hurt to swing past there on my way back to Ralph's house.

The GPS on my phone provided me with directions to the address I found in the people's search. It was an apartment complex composed of two and three-story brick buildings. I cruised through the parking lot, trying to avoid attention as my eyes scanned the lot for the SUV I had seen at Bolton's offices the day before. On my third pass, I spotted the blue behemoth.

I found an empty parking spot just two cars down from Jason's SUV. My next challenge would be to examine the car without getting noticed and perhaps being shot as a robber. The walking boot on my left foot made it hard to move around with aplomb. If someone spotted me, I was dead meat.

Crawling out of my rental and staying low to avoid detection, I again examined the front bumper of the SUV. The darkness made it more difficult to see, but the white paint from his collision with Jessica's AMG was still visible to the naked eye. On the opposite side of the bumper, I noticed another set of paint streaks. It was likely the result of the second bump we had experienced during the chase. I used the flashlight on my phone to inspect the marks. Using my pocket knife, I scraped a little of the paint into my handkerchief. If testing proved it was the same paint as Jessica's AMG, that would be all the proof we needed to implicate Callahan.

I crawled back to my rental car and started the engine just as a security patrol cruised down the aisle only two rows away from where I parked. I could not afford to get caught snooping around in a private parking lot. It was time to return to the Dowden residence.

As I turned back west, away from Needham Hills, a rush of excitement surged through my body. This investigation was likely the most thrilling detective work I experienced in the ten years since I began spying on people for money. When this investigation was finished and I was safely back in my office in Berwyn, Illinois – God willing – I would remember the feeling of this moment and log it in my journal.

* * *

I struggled to sleep that night. The excitement of crawling around in the dark, and the fear of getting caught trying to gather evidence from Callahan's car still had me keyed up.

As I tossed and turned, I kept replaying Tiffany Burns' statement in my head. During her initial interrogation, she lied about being at work the entire time. She was covering up her actions. I believed she was telling the truth when she said that she found Barry dead and just left the scene. A woman scorned is a prime candidate for a crime of passion. But her assertion that Barry was worth more to her alive than dead made sense. The question was one of emotion. Was she capable of controlling her emotions in the face of Barry's cheating and lies? Most women would want revenge.

Two days ago, Hale stated if we find more evidence, "All bets are off". There was more evidence to collect, but I was ready to place my bet against Sarah Thomas or her son Jason Callahan. If nothing else, I wanted to prove Callahan was the one who fired the shot that caused Jessica and me to run off the road.

We had to keep digging until the ballistics test confirmed or denied whether the bullets from the two crimes matched.

DIGGING DEEP

The next morning, I woke up early, eager to resume the investigation. I could smell freshly brewed coffee whiffing up the staircase from Ralph's kitchen. By the time I got down the stairs, Ralph was tossing a skillet full of scrambled eggs onto plates and pulling golden slices of toast from his toaster.

"Any word from Hale?" I asked.

"Not yet. What time did you get in?"

"A little after ten. I found Jason Callahan's car. I may have retrieved evidence that proves he was the one that ran us off the road. It may show it was his bullet that caused the crash."

"We should let Hale know," he said.

"Let's eat. If he doesn't contact us soon, could you send him a text?"

We ate our breakfast in relative silence, each one of us contemplating our next moves. The case was growing more complicated. Tiffany Burns had all but implicated Sarah Thomas in a conspiracy to frame Burns for Barry's demise. Was it all a smokescreen? Could there be someone else involved? Could it be Wallace Bolton, the individual with a huge incentive for Barry's demise? I wondered. "What about Bolton?"

Ralph hesitated to repeat it, but he still endorsed the possibility that Hale was correct from the beginning. Jessica killed her husband and framed Tiffany Burns. Jessica stood to inherit a fortune. She had the most to gain from Barry's death. Dowden always believed money was the chief motive in these spousal killings. Now that I could navigate on my own, we could explore two separate lines of thinking. Ralph planned to do his own research on Jessica McGleam.

After breakfast, I volunteered to wash the dishes. Ralph left the kitchen and headed upstairs to take a shower. The day ahead promised to be a busy one.

By the time Ralph reached the top of the stairs, I finished drying the dishes. I bolted for the office to begin my analysis of the data files I collected from Bolton's network. Ralph wasn't big on my searching for evidence obtained without proper authorization. He liked to keep things legitimate.

There were a lot of suspects in this investigation, but my primary goal was still to prove Jessica's innocence.

My raw data collection yielded hundreds of files, most of which were system logs or error files. It took me some time before I found the directories that were assigned to Bolton's staff members. The main directory contained copies of his campaign propaganda, nothing nefarious there. Browsing Bolton's directory proved to be a repeat of his social media posts. It was all about kissing babies and petting puppies.

Going down the list, I came to a directory that appeared to house files placed by Sarah Thomas. Most of the data was mundane, meeting minutes or dates and times of activities. Until I found one that I couldn't access. It was password-protected. The thought that she secured this directory intrigued me. I made several failed attempts to crack the password, but nothing I tried worked.

I was scratching my way through a list of terms I hoped would give me access to the file when Ralph entered the office.

"Looks like you're hard at it already," he said.

"Last night, I went over to Bolton's HQ and accessed his Wi-Fi. I downloaded a bunch of files."

Ralph shook his head. "You will never be able to use that evidence in a court of law. In fact, you committed a crime by collecting the data without permission. I think you are getting too involved in this case."

It was the first time Ralph and I disagreed. "Just let me view this one directory. It belongs to Sarah Thomas, but it is password-protected. I have tried several, but nothing seems to work."

"Body, do you know how hard it is to crack a password without some sort of supercomputer? Nearly impossible."

"I know, but people use simple passwords they can remember. I tried 'Sarah123' and 'SThomas123' and a few others."

Ralph didn't say another word. Instead, he sat down at his computer and started typing. I knew we were supposed to revisit Stoney Brook this morning, but I sidetracked us.

After about ten minutes, Ralph said, "Try this for a password. '02051971'."

"What is that?" I asked.

"It's Sarah Thomas' birthday."

Once again, Ralph solved the mystery. The password worked. The directory contained twenty-two photo images. Two pictures captured Barry McGleam at a public location, likely during a campaign visit. All the others were of Tiffany Burns, including several racy photos of Barry and Tiffany Burns together, like the ones I had seen on social media weeks before. Most disturbing were two photos of Tiffany topless on stage. In one, she was bent over, flashing her shapely buttocks clothed only in a G-string. In the other, she had her leg wrapped around a pole, her breasts in full display. Around her feet lay a pile of five and ten-dollar bills tossed on stage by club patrons. Those two pictures clearly violated The Peppermint Lounge's no-photography policy. Whoever took those pictures took the risk of dealing with the club's bouncers if caught.

I couldn't help but feel she was planning something evil, but what? I browsed the images again, trying to imagine why Sarah was collecting images of Tiffany and Barry, many of which were publicly available on social media, when Ralph's phone chimed.

"I just got a text from Hale. His detectives are bringing in Sarah Thomas and Jason Callahan for questioning. We need to put this on hold for now."

"Okay, let's get over there. I'll drive," I said.

En route to police headquarters, I couldn't get those naked images of Tiffany Burns out of my head. I always believed that Jessica was one of the most beautiful women I knew. After seeing Tiffany on stage, I understood how Barry McGleam could fall under the spell of this femme fatale.

Ralph sensed my thoughts because he said to me, "Able, you need to pull back and let Hale do his job. Stealing those files from Bolton's office will be your Watergate. Don't let it happen. At least for now, keep it in your back pocket."

I wanted to argue, but Ralph was right. I was pushing too hard to find the bad guy. We needed hard evidence, not more circumstantial evidence. The case was getting complicated. It was getting too easy to get sidetracked.

We arrived at police headquarters in about twenty minutes. Once again, we informed the desk sergeant that Hale requested us to view a lineup. Those keywords allowed us to enter the secure area of the police station. I wondered how long we could use that ruse before someone would ask us more in-depth questions. On our way upstairs, we passed Lieutenant Hale's desk. He was on the phone and waved us on toward the observation room.

Sarah Thomas sat nervously at the table with a surprise accompaniment: Wallace Bolton. Bolton was there, acting as her legal representative.

A few minutes later, Hale stepped into the observation room. Motioning with his hand to stay calm, he whispered to Ralph and me.

"Keep your voices down. This guy Bolton is a sharp cookie. We need to tread lightly. They don't know we have Jason Callahan detained in another room. I have a forensics team going over Callahan's SUV with a fine-tooth comb."

Both Ralph and I nodded our understanding of the situation. As Hale left the room, I pumped my fist with excitement. After days of stonewalling, Hale's view of the situation turned to a more open-minded stance. He was finally assuming a more aggressive response.

I watched as Bolton and Thomas bantered back and forth, trying to align their thinking. Bolton cautioned her to keep her responses simple.

Hale entered with a substantial paper file, nearly an inch thick, in his hands. He slammed the folder on the desk in an intimidating fashion.

His bold inquiry took Thomas by surprise. "Where were you last Tuesday evening?"

She stammered, "Tuesday? Let me think."

"It's not that difficult a question," Hale snapped.

"I was at the campaign office."

Hale's eyes shifted to Bolton. "Can you vouch for her, Mr. Bolton?"

Bolton, a veteran of criminal prosecutions, flashed an angry look at Hale. "I am not the one you should be questioning."

"All I asked is if you can verify her alibi. I believe you had an event at your office that night."

Hale had set a trap. If Bolton confirmed her alibi when evidence showed she may have left the building, he would end up with an egg on his face.

Bolton sidestepped his question. "Direct your questions to Ms. Thomas."

Hale tightened the noose. "Ms. Thomas, did you leave the campaign office any time between the hours of 7:00 pm and 10:00 pm?"

Suspecting Hale knew more than he was revealing, she said. "I had an errand to run. I had to pick up some campaign literature."

Able thought for sure Hale would probe deeper into where she went. Instead, he shifted gears. "Do you own a gun?"

"Yes, it was my husband's. I kept it when he was incarcerated. I keep it in a locked drawer in my home office."

"What kind of gun is it?" asked Hale.

"I don't know. I am not that knowledgeable about guns. A handgun of some sort."

"Who has access to the weapon?"

"No one. Only me," she said.

"We'll need to see the gun and perform some ballistics tests."

Bolton piped in. "As soon as you present a warrant, my client will comply."

"We are awaiting the delivery of a search warrant. It should be here shortly."

Without uttering a word, Hale stood and exited the room. His abrupt and random questioning had caught Thomas and Bolton off guard. They looked at each other with curious looks on their faces.

Bolton tried to calm Sarah down by saying, "He's got nothing. He's just trying to confuse us."

From the sound of Bolton's voice, Hale's questions had thrown off his confidence. Bolton could not vouch for Thomas without involving himself. Any implication that Bolton was somehow involved in Barry McGleam's death would hamper his bid for election. Bolton's expression revealed his regret for accompanying Sarah to the police station. He should have sent another attorney, not one running for public office, to help her.

It made me wonder if Bolton's presence was an attempt to cover his own ass by claiming attorney-client privilege as a way of keeping Sarah Thomas from implicating him.

It seemed like Lieutenant Hale was gone longer than necessary. Peeking out the observation room door, I cautiously checked if he was at his desk. I couldn't see Hale anywhere.

"What do you think he is doing?" I asked Ralph.

"Beats me. Maybe he is questioning Callahan. He's probably trying to play one against another."

We sat together in silence, waiting another thirty minutes. Suddenly, Hale burst into the interrogation room again.

Again, he took an aggressive posture. Nearly shouting, he asked. "We discovered paint matching that of Jessica McGleam's AMG on the front bumper of Jason Callahan's SUV. Wanna tell me how it got there?"

Sarah responded, "You'll have to ask Jason. He's not a very good driver."

"Did you know he ran Jessica McGleam and her associate off the road near the Stoney Brook Wildlife Area? He fled the scene of the accident."

"Why tell me? I wasn't with him," she said.

"I thought you might like to know; I plan to charge Jason with Vehicular Manslaughter. He faces a lengthy jail sentence. Looks like he's following in his father's footsteps."

"Jessica's dead?" she asked.

Sarah looked at Bolton. "You said he was only going to scare her."

Bolton turned white as a ghost. "Shut up Sarah. Limit your answers to yes or no," he advised.

Visibly upset by Hale's revelation, she snapped at Bolton. "Wallace, you're fired. You suck."

Then she turned toward Lieutenant Hale. "Get me another lawyer. A public defender, I don't care."

Hale couldn't help cracking a smile. "I thought he was your lawyer?"

"Mr. Bolton, it seems you have been dismissed. Please see your way out. Oh, and don't leave town. I will have some questions for you."

"I'm not going anywhere," screamed Bolton.

"Then I will charge you with obstructing justice and hold you here until we sort this whole mess out."

With no legal justification to remain, Bolton angrily stormed from the room.

Hale looked at Sarah Thomas. "Now Ms. Thomas, let's start at the beginning."

Sarah's face turned red with anger. Confused and unsure, she sought Hale's advice. "Am I under arrest?"

"Should you be?"

"If you are not charging me. I want to leave."

"I am going to hold you here until your new attorney comes. I suggest you relax. Would you like a coffee or soda?"

Sarah Thomas' comment to Wallace Bolton piqued Hale's interest. His previously smooth investigation appeared to be taking on a life of its own. It made me wonder, "Was Bolton the mastermind behind Barry McGleam's death?"

Little did Thomas know; Jessica was still clinging to life in her hospital bed.

* * *

While Sarah Thomas awaited the arrival of a new public defender, Hale returned to his desk. He had two more tasks ahead. One, the questioning of Jason Callahan, hoping to gain evidence that proved Barry McGleam's murder, and the attempt on Jessica's life were coordinated events. His second task was finding the murder weapon. He instructed another detective on his team to pursue a search warrant for Sarah Thomas's house. He wanted to inspect her gun.

Having nothing left to observe, Ralph and I looked at each other and shrugged. It was time to leave police headquarters and ponder our next move.

It was then I had a bright idea. A CSI team never examined the accident scene where Jessica and I were pushed off the road by Callahan. The law enforcement officers who responded to the crash treated it as a traffic accident. I wanted to examine the crash site more closely. I convinced Ralph to drive back to the Stoney Brook Wildlife Area and together we would search the area for clues.

"Don't you think we would be better off waiting until morning? That area is quite rural. It is dark and desolate, and the road is winding. We may not find the crash spot again. If we wait until sunup, we can see what we are doing."

"You're probably right, but there will be a lot less traffic at night. The crash site may be difficult to examine during the day due to the constant flow of passing cars. If you don't want to go, I'll go alone. Let me borrow a flashlight."

With no way to stop me, Ralph reluctantly agreed to join me.

We drove slowly down the narrow roadway, stopping occasionally to observe several places where it looked like cars had stopped along the route. We finally found the crash site as evidenced by the twisted metal guard rail and still visible deep tire tracks left in the dirt by Jessica's AMG.

"This is it," I declared. "Let's get a better look."

Still sporting a walking boot, I limped along the roadway, diligently shining a flashlight at suspicious objects. Ralph paced ahead a hundred feet past the crash site and panned the area, looking for clues.

"I can't see anything. It's too dark to see anything," he said.

Frustrated by not finding any clues, I conceded our chances of finding any evidence in the dark were slim. The darkness and time that had elapsed since the accident made the odds unfavorable.

I conceded Ralph was right, but added a caveat, "Okay, but I want to try again tomorrow in the daylight."

Before departing the area, we cruised slowly down the deserted road, searching for anything unusual. That's when Ralph noticed something amiss.

About two hundred yards past the crash site, he spotted a section where the grass and trees looked trampled. We scanned the highway, curious about the contrasting patch of trampled ground.

"Look here," he said. "Something strange happened here. It looks like a car drove through here. The driver probably tried turning around and pulled in too far off the pavement. Look, there are tire marks. A car was stuck. They rocked the car to get it out of the gravel."

Using the headlights from my rental car, we scanned the spot that Ralph pointed out. He had a lead, but it was still too dark to gather evidence.

"Able, this will not work. Mark this spot with the GPS on your phone. We should return in the morning for further investigation. We'll take pictures and possibly discover something useful."

Reluctantly, I agreed. It had been a long day. Now, knowing more evidence awaited us, it was going to be a longer night.

What I didn't know was Lieutenant Hale had a couple of aces up his sleeve. Besides having Sarah Thomas in the interrogation room, he already requested a search warrant for both her house and Jason Callahan's apartment.

Little by little, with my and Ralph's help, Hale was piecing together a scenario that explained the complex series of events leading up to and after Barry's death. Despite pressure from the District Attorney's office, Hale was holding off on charging anyone until he was sure the evidence supported his actions.

Tommy Boyle wanted blood, demanding action. Hale wanted to avoid an O.J. Simpson type of trial.

A RETURN TO THE SCENE

I tossed and turned all night. Sleeping in a strange bed with noises like dogs barking, trees rustling, and unfamiliar house sounds woke me up several times during the night. I was beginning to long for my own bed and the comfortable monotony of Berwyn.

Still, with Ralph's help, I made a convert out of Hale. He was looking into our evidence. Now, collectively, we needed to follow through and solve this murder mystery.

When morning rolled around, I hobbled into Ralph's kitchen, still tired. While I made a fresh pot of coffee. I could hear the water running upstairs. Ralph was already awake and showering.

Before I could pop two slices of bread into the toaster, Ralph came downstairs, ready for action.

"Smells good," he said.

"Butter or jam?" I asked.

"Both. I'll grab some of that fruit salad I bought at the grocery store the other day. It should still be good."

I poured the coffee while Ralph laid out some plates and silverware.

Ralph scooped a generous helping of fruit salad into bowls.

"As soon as we finish here, we need to go back to Stoney Brook. We might still find something there," Ralph said.

While we buttered our toast, we each pondered how this reexamination of the crash site might turn out.

"Do you have a metal detector?" I asked.

"Of course, what self-respecting P.I. doesn't?"

"Bring it with you. Oh, bring a tape measure, too. I'd like to inspect the location we were at last night. The spot where it looks like someone turned a car around. Bring a couple of plastic bags as well, in case we find something."

He shrugged his shoulders. "Finding anything meaningful is a long shot. It's been a week. The weather and heavy traffic may compromise the evidence on the road."

"Have you got anything better to do today?" I asked.

With no argument to defend, he said. "I'll be in the garage. Metal detector, tape measure, flashlights, gloves. What else?"

"Bring your good luck charm," I said.

* * *

Thirty minutes later, we arrived at the bend in the road just north of the Stoney Brook Wildlife Sanctuary. I instructed Ralph to keep driving to the location we visited last night, just two hundred yards further down the road from the crash site.

Carefully, we surveyed the area around the spot that I marked on my phone with the GPS app. Ralph identified this location as the area used by a car to turn around. He was on target. Despite the passing days, the tracks from the evening of the crash remained visible.

"You were right. Someone tried to turn around here. They went too far past the gravel apron," I said.

The car's front tires had plowed through a dirt embankment built up to prevent cars from veering into the woods. The car's rear tires left deep ruts in the soft ground as the driver attempted to free it from the ditch.

Examining the markings, I had a flashback. The car that cruised past me seconds after the crash and the one that turned around here were the same car. The driver who drove past our crash wasn't there to help. He wanted us dead.

It was my turn to take the lead in this investigation. Ralph had the experience, but through my internships here in Massachusetts and in Illinois, I sharpened my skills as a forensic investigator. From the conditions at this scene, we could gather enough evidence to reconstruct Jason Callahan's actions during the pursuit and crash.

I instructed Ralph, "Get the tape measure and measure the distance between where the front tires went over the edge and the marks left by the rear tires. That information will reveal the car's wheelbase. Then measure the width between the front wheels. Likewise, measure the width between the rear wheels. While you do that, I'll capture photographs to verify the measurements."

Ralph followed my instructions, measuring and noting each spot.

I snapped pictures that showed the measurements Ralph made at each point of the turnaround site. He sketched a crude drawing on a notepad. When he finished, you could envision the distance between the car's tires and the outline of the shape of the automobile's body.

Then Ralph noticed something else. "Look at this," Ralph said. He pointed toward the base of a tree immediately in front of where the car stopped. "This tree is showing damage. It's recent. Probably from the car's bumper." Rocking the car back and forth, the driver broke a chunk of bark away from the tree trunk.

I told Ralph. "Measure that spot as well. Measure from the spot where the front tire tracks were left on the ground to the tree trunk. It gives us an idea of the distance from the front tire to the bumper. Also, measure from the ground up to the mark on the trunk. Let's see if it matches the height of the bumper of Jason's SUV."

Ralph tried to temper his excitement. He hadn't performed in-depth detective work in years. This case gave him the opportunity for a meaningful contribution in a criminal investigation. He recognized the significance of every piece of evidence, no matter how small, in potentially uncovering a breakthrough.

"I don't think we can prove it was Jason's SUV that made these marks. I'm guessing there are a thousand cars with these dimensions in the Boston area," he said.

"You're right. It is circumstantial. We need more," I said.

I looked around at the roadway and the ground surrounding the vehicle's outline. The area was so badly trampled that it was impossible to find any unspoiled footprints. Once again, I envisioned myself as a brilliant detective in the spirit of Hercule Poirot or Sherlock Holmes. "How would a famous detective solve this mystery?" I thought.

I tried to visualize the driver's actions. I limped to the front of the car, mimicking the driver's stance as if surveying the damage. Then another thought popped into my head.

"Let's see, a nine-millimeter Glock pistol weighs about twenty-five ounces," I said.

I grabbed a stone about the same size and weight as a typical handgun. I tossed it as far as I could into the woods.

Pointing to a spot about thirty feet away, I postulated. "If Callahan tossed the gun into the trees, that's the area where it would land."

Ralph challenged my thinking. "Are you serious? Do you believe he got rid of the gun out there?"

"Serious as a heart attack," I chuckled.

Shrugging my shoulders, I said. "Besides, I haven't anything else to do today. I wanna go out there and explore a bit."

Taking the tape measure from Ralph's hand. I handed the open end to Ralph. "Hold this end of the tape measure. I'm going in there."

Out I went, walking boot and all. I hobbled into the trees with Ralph's metal detector firmly in my grip. When I arrived at the spot close to where the rock landed, I called out. "Thirty-three feet. Write that down. I'm going to survey the area in a thirty-three-foot arc. Maybe we will find something."

I paced around, swinging the metal detector over the ground, back and forth in a three-foot-wide pathway, mimicking a tutorial video I had seen on how to use a metal detector. I worked slowly so as not to miss any areas. Back and forth, section by section, I surveyed the ground. At first, all I kept locating were little pieces of scrap metal and rusted cans.

Like a man possessed, I hobbled back and forth on the uneven ground, almost falling several times because of the walking boot on my foot.

Ralph watched, wondering if we were wasting our time. Perhaps it would be better for Lieutenant Hale and the Norfolk County detectives to handle the case.

Just when I was about to give up on my crazy idea, the metal detector beeped alarmingly.

"I got something!" I cried.

I brushed away a pile of twigs with my hand. There it was, a handgun, partially buried beneath the leaves. The gun seemed too clean and fresh to have been there long. Whoever discarded it, did it in the last few days.

I took the tape measure and guided it around the trees and bushes until I could get an accurate measurement above the spot where the gun was lying.

"Thirty-six feet. Callahan had a powerful throwing arm."

Ralph couldn't believe I found the murder weapon. Or at least a handgun. One that might be the murder weapon.

"Call Hale. Tell him we may have found the murder weapon," I called out.

Ralph dialed Lieutenant Hale's telephone number. There was no answer.

From across the weeds, I yelled, "Try again. Keep trying, maybe they're busy."

Ralph dialed again. This time, one of the detectives on Hale's team answered. "This is Detective O'Hara."

Ralph held up his thumb signaling success. He spoke into the phone. "I need to get a message to Lieutenant Hale. It is about a case he is working on. Barry McGleam's death. I think we found the murder weapon."

"Who is this?" he asked.

"Ralph Dowden, a private investigator who is looking into the case. Hale knows me."

There was a pause. "Where are you?"

Out on Route 115, just north of the Stoney Brook Wildlife Sanctuary. Near a street called Needham. I don't know the mile marker.

"Don't touch anything. I am sending a patrol officer," he said.

Just to be sure, Ralph texted Lieutenant Hale's cell phone, informing him of the series of events. Hale did not immediately reply. Whatever he was doing was keeping him busy.

Ralph and I had no choice but to wait. Rather than stand out in the brush with the bugs and blooming poison ivy, I marked the spot using a tree branch and rejoined Ralph at the side of the roadway. It took approximately fifteen minutes for a patrol car to arrive at the scene. The young officer with olive skin and dark hair climbed out of his car. His badge displayed his name, A. Salvadoni, and I remembered his badge number was 68432. He looked at me and Ralph pacing around.

"Did one of you guys make a call to the precinct?"

Ralph introduced us and explained how we were working with Lieutenant Hale. He pointed to the section of the road siding where the car turned around. He showed Salvadoni the sketches he made of the scene. Standing near the spot where I estimated the driver stood and explained how we measured the distance to the gun.

Salvadoni jotted down the location and time, snapping pictures with his phone of the location and terrain. Then, grabbing a pair of gloves and an evidence bag, he followed me out to the spot where the gun lay in the grass.

Snapping a picture of the spot I marked with the tree branch, he looked around for something he could use to pick up the gun without compromising any potential fingerprints. Using a twig, he picked up the weapon and dropped it into the evidence bag.

"I'll get this to one of Lieutenant Hale's detectives ASAP," he said.

Before Salvadoni left, he allowed me to take close-up pictures of the gun through the clear plastic evidence bag. Even though it was heading to the crime lab, I hoped to use the pictures to match the gun we found to Barry's murder weapon.

With the gun safely in possession of the Norfolk County police, Ralph and I headed back to Natick. We wouldn't hear anything for a few hours.

On the way home, I examined the pictures I had taken of the gun. It matched pictures of a nine-millimeter Glock 48 semi-automatic pistol. According to a description I found on the internet, the gun had a ten-shot magazine. Ten shots, more than enough to commit two crimes. In one picture, my eye glimpsed at what looked like a spot where the gun's serial number should be. It looked like someone welded over the spot to hinder tracing. In the area where the serial number belonged, someone crudely scratched the word REVENGE into the metal.

Most likely, the person who tossed the gun had wiped the outside of it clean of any fingerprints in an attempt to conceal their identity. If true, that meant the crime was premeditated. The Norfolk County forensics team was now tasked with trying to identify the shooter using whatever little evidence they could gather from the weapon.

Back in Natick, Ralph made lunch while I searched the internet trying to discover more about the gun. At the Stoney Brook site, we found a mountain of evidence that needed to be reviewed by the crime lab.

Collectively, we sat on pins and needles, awaiting the results of the Norfolk County forensic team's crime scene testing. I felt confident the evidence we uncovered proved beyond a shadow of a doubt that Jason Callahan instigated the crash that put Jessica and me in the hospital. Still, a bigger question remained. Would the evidence also tie him to Barry McGleam's death?

We were just sitting down to eat when the doorbell rang. Ralph looked at me. I glanced back at him.

"Are you expecting anyone?" I asked.

"No, it's probably someone selling something. I'll get it," said Ralph.

Ralph gazed through the peephole. A young man paced nervously in circles outside Ralph's front door. He held in his hands two manila envelopes. Ralph swung the door open, startling the messenger.

"Mr. Dowden?" he asked.

Ralph knew what he wanted. He had served many subpoenas as a sideline when he first started the investigative business. "Yes, I am Ralph Dowden."

The young man handed him one envelope. "Sir, the District Attorney's office has subpoenaed you. I understand you have a Mr. Bōdyē at this address as well?"

I stepped up to the door next to Ralph.

Handing me the second envelope, he repeated. "Mr. Bōdyē, the District Attorney's office, has subpoenaed you. Gentlemen, consider yourself served."

The subpoenas required Ralph and I to appear tomorrow at 2:00 p.m. and 2:30 p.m., respectively, to be deposed in the matter of Barry McGleam's murder.

"We'd better call a lawyer," Ralph said.

"Why do we need a lawyer?"

"You heard Hale questioning Sarah, didn't you? These guys get tricky. They make you say stuff you didn't mean to say. Better to be safe than sorry."

"Do you know anybody?" I asked.

"Yes, I know a good criminal defense lawyer named Paul Braun. I'll call him after lunch."

Ralph and I met Paul Braun, the next day, at the offices of the District Attorney in Canton, MA. About fifteen miles from Ralph's house.

Ralph was the first to be deposed. According to Ralph, the attorney conducting the deposition, Michael Flanagan, kept the questions civil and non-threatening. Flanagan was used to working with private investigators. He only wanted to understand Ralph's involvement in the case, but more importantly, he wanted to know Ralph's relationship with Able Body. Ralph had been through the process before, only offering as much information as necessary.

"I hired Mr. Body as a consultant. He's younger and has excellent computer skills," stated Ralph.

When Flanagan cautioned Ralph that his actions could have compromised a murder investigation, Ralph reminded him that without our involvement, the D.A.'s office would have charged Jessica McGleam with murder. The actual killers would have gotten away.

Flanagan conceded the point and thanked Ralph for his assistance. Ralph was in and out of his deposition in twenty minutes. A relaxed and confident Ralph Dowden updated me on his interview.

"They just wanted my statement regarding how I got involved with the case. Pretty straightforward. I don't think they will be as easy with you. They're angry about an Illinois detective snooping around Massachusetts."

When my turn came, I slipped into a seat next to Paul Braun hoping Flanagan would go as easy on me as he had on Ralph. He didn't. Almost instantly his demeanor changed. Toward me, he became aggressive and argumentative. The lack of reciprocity agreements between Illinois and Massachusetts meant I should not be working in Norfolk County. In Flanagan's opinion, I skirted the law by involving Ralph Dowden.

"You came here knowing any actions you performed would be illegal. You could have jeopardized the entire murder investigation.

We will be lucky if the judge doesn't throw the evidence, you two collected out the window."

Trying to remain calm, I argued, "Everything Ralph did, and everything I did with him, was legal and above board. Mr. Dowden hired me as a research assistant. I have invoiced Mr. Dowden for my time and expenses."

I could sense a bit of resentment from the Norfolk County D.A.'s office. Flanagan and his fellow associates had developed a close relationship with Barry McGleam, their future boss. His death angered them. Attorneys, particularly District Attorneys, have become targets of bad guys. Barry's murder was a reminder that their good-guy image was being tested.

Although contentious, the deposition went as planned. I held nothing back in painting the picture of a revenge murder by people who wanted Barry dead. I stressed the point that Jessica McGleam had more to lose with Barry dead than alive.

After explaining my relationship with Jessica. Then, how Ralph and I found the bullet hole in Jessica's car and how we obtained the video showing Tiffany Burns leaving the Peppermint Lounge, Flanagan backed off a little. He took my statement, noting the sequence of events and the details of each discovery.

By the end of the deposition, Flanagan's posture changed to one of gratitude. I felt vindicated.

During the deposition, I received a phone call. In silent mode, my phone buzzed in my pocket. I ignored the call and let it go to voicemail. When I left the District Attorney's office, I met again with Ralph.

"Flanagan read me the riot act. Don't worry, I got thick skin," I declared. "Looks like I got a phone call from George Sekelsky. He left a message: Jessica's awake. After we're done here, I need to go to the hospital."

We had a quick meeting with Paul Braun to ensure the depositions were satisfactory. He directed us to sit tight. Flanagan suggested the next few days were going to be significant. He felt several arrests were forthcoming.

I high-tailed it from Canton, down to Norfolk, where Jessica was still being treated. I arrived at Jessica's hospital to learn they had moved her out of intensive care. That was a good sign.

When I entered her room, Jessica looked at me and offered a weak smile. Her face looked drawn; her eyes were tired. She immediately tried to fuss with her hair in a discomfited manner. Her lips, still dried and cracked from the breathing tube, looked raw. Her former rich and supple skin took on an almost colorless patina.

George and Marian Sekelsky sat watching television, but as soon as they saw me, they greeted me. Without being asked, they left the room. They wanted Jessica and I, two would-be lovers, to be alone.

"Jessica, you look beautiful," I said.

"You always say that. I know I look like shit. I feel like hell. The doctors say it will be weeks of therapy before I can walk again. Right now, I am so full of painkillers I can't feel anything."

"Don't worry, we'll get there. I'll stay with you until you can come home again."

Jessica changed the subject. "How are you doing? I don't remember too much after that car chased us." She looked at the still unhealed wound on my forehead. "My parents told me you were hurt pretty badly in the accident. Are you alright?"

"Apart from this," I pointed to the walking boot that still cradled my foot. "And this," I rubbed the stitches on my forehead. "I am almost fully recovered."

Then I got back on topic. "I have a lot to tell you."

"Did they find out who killed Barry?" she asked.

"We are working on it. Remember Ralph Dowden, the Private Investigator I worked for back in college? He has been helping me and the police."

"That's what I understand. I'm sorry, I don't remember him. It was a long time ago."

She continued to fuss with her hair, trying to regain a small amount of her former youthful splendor.

I sat next to her and took her hand. We didn't have much to say to each other. Each one tried to generate small talk but realized the only thing we had to talk about was the doctors, our injuries, and the night of the crash.

After a few minutes, Jessica fell back asleep, and I stood by watching her, watching the host of electrical machines, tubes and wires still connected to her.

I stayed with her until visiting hours were over, then kissed her good night. Then I drove slowly back to Ralph's house. Once more, I pondered the purpose behind it all. Barry's murder, mine and Jessica's near-death experiences, and a police investigation that will probably result in a life sentence for one or more people. It was the type of big drama that seemed to follow Jessica around. I never cared much for the drama, preferring a low-key, easy lifestyle. I was missing Berwyn and Thelma Jenkins. I missed my old mid-century office with its wooden doors and creaky floors and a window view of the train station across the street. Despite our unfinished business in Boston, my heart told me it was time to return home.

I spent another uneasy night of sleep at Ralph's. Hale had all the puzzle pieces on the table. I knew he would arrest and charge someone for both Barry's murder and the near-fatal road rage incident that nearly killed Jessica and me. The question was, would he successfully piece the puzzle together and reach the right result?

IF NOT TIFFANY, THEN WHO

The next morning, Ralph and I met with Lieutenant Hale at his desk for an update. The lieutenant had been hard at work.

His attitude toward the two private investigators was mellowing. In the beginning, we were a pain in his ass. Since then, the circumstances have changed. The case turned out to be more than a simple domestic quarrel that went badly, much more. He realized, without our insistence, the wrong person might have gone to jail.

He also knew we were helping. Whenever Ralph and I added a new piece to the puzzle, Hale would confirm its fit with their previous evidence. That meant more work for him.

The gun that we found was fresh evidence. He had just received the report from forensics. It was lying atop his desk. He picked it up and started reviewing it with us.

"Ballistics matched the gun you found with the bullets CSI found in Jessica's car and the two that killed Barry McGleam. That gun is definitely the murder weapon. Sarah claimed she had that gun, Larry's gun, locked up in a drawer at her house. We know now that was a lie.

"The shooter wiped the gun clean before they tossed it into the woods. The moisture and dirt from the grass made it impossible to find any usable prints on the outside casing. The ten-shot magazine showed the shooter emptied four shots from the magazine. We know that two went into Barry. Two into Jessica's car.

"Forensics found two partial prints on the inside of the gun. One on the magazine and one on a shell casing. When we tried to match it up with Jason Callahan's or Sarah Thomas' prints, neither one matched."

"Too bad. I hoped for a match," I said.

"Wait, you haven't heard the best part. Our forensic officer pushed it into the FBI national database, looking for any match. Her hard work paid off. A match came up. It matched Larry Callahan, Jason's father.

"Either way, it ties Sarah and Jason to both your car crash and Barry McGleam's death. We pulled a search warrant for Jason's apartment. The place was a pigsty. He had soiled clothes, empty beer bottles, garbage, and dirty dishes all over the place.

"Forensics is testing some clothes they found on the floor for gunshot residue. If they find it, we will have our killer within a shadow of a doubt.

"I'm crossing my fingers," I said.

"Either way, I am arresting Jason for Barry's murder. I am just trying to piece together how Sarah Thomas, Tiffany Burns, and maybe Wallace Bolton are all involved. I can't stop thinking they had some kind of conspiracy going on. I'm still unsure about who did what."

I asked Hale, "Can we observe again? Maybe we can pick out some clues during the interrogation?"

Hale looked at his watch. "I was going to grab a sandwich. I should have Tiffany Burns here in a room as soon as one of my team members can locate her. She'll probably lawyer up again. Then I am going to bring in Sarah Thomas again for questioning. Come back in about an hour. We will probably have one of them here again."

* * *

An hour later, Ralph and I were back in the Norfolk County police station. Seated at the interrogation table were Tiffany Burns and her lawyer, Robert Semtack. Burns wasn't happy about being pulled back into the police station.

"Why am I here again? I told you everything I know. I will make just one statement for the record. I didn't kill Barry McGleam," she said.

Hale knew Tiffany didn't kill Barry. He also knew she wasn't telling the whole story. Tiffany knew facts that might impact the investigation.

"Last time you were here, you lied to me, Ms. Burns. You stated that when you went to Barry's offices, he was already dead. You said you didn't touch anything inside, that you left immediately. Would you like to reconsider your previous statement?"

Tiffany looked at Semtack. "I need to confer with my client," said Semtack.

"Take your time, we both get paid by the hour," chirped Hale.

Semtack and Burns whispered to each other, and then Tiffany nodded.

"My client wants to amend her earlier statement. "There might have been confusion," Semtack said.

"There isn't any confusion, Mr. Semtack. I have her statement on videotape," said Hale. "But Ms. Burns, if you feel you have more to say, amend away."

Tiffany shifted in her seat. "Okay, it was true when I got there Barry was already lying on the floor. I could see the pool of blood; from the amount of blood loss, I knew he was dead. I used my purse to push the door open so I wouldn't leave any fingerprints. There was no one else around. I didn't want him lying there all night. There was nothing I could do, so I walked to the desk. I took the phone off the hook and used a pen to dial 911. I ran out of there as fast as I could. I figured the police would sort it all out."

While Tiffany's story fit in with Hale's theory, he had more questions.

"Why did Sarah Thomas call you? What made you go to Barry's, to begin with?" he asked.

"Don't you see? It was a setup. Sarah knew Barry was going to dump me. When she called me to tell me Barry was with another girl, she was lighting the fuse. Like a dummy, I fell for it. Sarah set me up. She figured you guys would make me for the murder, not Jason."

Hale didn't want to accept Tiffany's response. "Are you aware that citizens have a duty to report a violent crime or death? I can have you charged with violation of state law."

"I did report it. I dialed 911. I just didn't stick around for the police to arrive."

It was semantics. Hale knew if her story panned out the worst that would happen to Tiffany would be a monetary fine. It wasn't worth charging her without more evidence.

Frustrated, Hale had no choice but to once again release Tiffany Burns. "Okay, Ms. Burns, you can go. But I plan to keep my eye on you."

Tiffany responded. "That's okay I'm used to being watched. Every night I have hundreds of men keeping their eyes on me. Half of them are like you, frustrated cops. Come by the Peppermint Lounge on Thursday, Friday, or Saturday after 8:00 p.m. I'll be there. You can keep your eyes on me as long as you like. But bring a handful of five-dollar bills."

Ralph looked at me. "She has a pretty solid alibi. I guess that's one suspect we can scratch off the list."

Deep in my mind, I still liked Tiffany Burns for Barry's death. Despite her alibi, I thought she might be hiding something more. To me, it just made sense. Under the circumstances, I had to concede my top suspect might go free.

✱ ✱ ✱

While we hashed over Tiffany Burn's latest statement, we waited to see who Hale scheduled next in the hot seat. Hale dragged Sarah Thomas into the interrogation room. Ballistics proved the gun that killed Barry and caused the crash of Jessica's car was owned by Sarah Thomas' former husband. She earlier testified she had locked that gun safely in a drawer at her house. When Hale executed a search of Sarah's house, the gun was no longer in her possession.

"Sarah, you have a great deal of explaining to do," said Hale.

He showed her two pictures of the gun we retrieved from the woods near Stoney Brook Wildlife Area.

"Recognize this?"

Sarah's reaction told the story. At first, she tried to deny it was hers.

"Should I?" she asked.

"It's the same gun you claimed you locked in a drawer at your residence. We found it near the crime scene."

Her lawyer, James Begley, looked closely at the pictures. "What proof have you got that this is Sarah's gun? The pictures clearly show they scratched the serial number off."

"The fingerprints on the magazine matched her husband, Larry Callahan. We know that Jason Callahan stopped his car thirty feet from where we found the gun. We also know Jason used his SUV to drive Jessica McGleam's car off the road at the sight of where the gun was found. By the way, the ballistics tests prove the bullets that caused Mrs. McGleam's accident and the bullets that killed Barry McGleam came from this gun."

James Begley looked at Sarah. Her face turned sad as the tears started flowing down her cheeks.

"It's over Sarah," declared Hale. "We have enough evidence to convict Jason and charge you as a co-conspirator."

"No!" Sarah screamed. "It wasn't Jason. It was me! I gave Jessica my gun. I saw Jessica shoot Barry McGleam. Then she ran away before I could stop her.

"I took Jason's car and chased her. I forced them off the road. She still had the gun in her possession. Her injuries were terrible, I knew she wouldn't survive. I took the gun away from Jessica and shot that Body guy. Then I placed the gun back into Jessica's hand. I thought that when you found the gun, you would blame her. I didn't mean for Jessica to die. When I chased them, I only wanted to run them off the road. It wasn't murder, it was a crime of passion. I confess."

Hale knew Sarah was fabricating a story to protect her son. "You mean you were the one that put the gun in Jessica's hand? You were the one who shot Able Body, Jessica's driver?"

"Yes, I shot him. I put the gun in Jessica's hand to make it look like she shot him. They were both dying anyway."

Sarah's impromptu attempt at a confession was nothing more than a ruse to keep Jason out of jail. Her husband, Larry, died in jail; she didn't want her son to die in jail like his father.

"Nice try, Sarah, except that's not how it happened. We found the gun in the woods. Oh, and Jessica McGleam is still alive. She is recovering in Norfolk County Medical Center Hospital."

"You son of a bitch, you said she was dead!" screamed Sarah.

"I never said she was dead. I said I would charge Jason with Vehicular Manslaughter. Based on new evidence, I am charging him with murder and attempted manslaughter."

Hale still didn't understand the interaction between Tiffany Burns and Sarah Thomas. I only have one question: "Why call Tiffany Burns?" Why did you call Tiffany and ask her to go to Barry's campaign offices? You had to know the police would suspect her."

Her eyes flamed with beams of hatred. "Tiffany is a whore. She dances in front of pathetic, lonely men, flashing her boobs and wiggling her ass while they stick money in her pants. Then she takes them to the back room and performs despicable acts with them. She wears expensive clothes and jewelry, then drives home in her expensive sports car. All bought with money from teasing horney old men. Tiffany Burns works for the devil.

"That's how she met Barry. He paid her to be his whore. My brother would be mortified if he knew how his daughter made a living. If he knew her history with men, he'd condemn her to hell."

Hale shook his head. "Your own niece. You tried to frame your own niece?"

Begley said, "Don't say another word, Sarah. You are only making things worse."

Without warning, Lieutenant Hale stood up and walked out of the room. I looked at Ralph. Motioning with my hands, I signaled. What's he doing? Ralph shrugged his shoulders. Hale's sudden exit confused us both.

Within three minutes, Hale answered our questions. A uniformed police officer accompanied Hale into the room.

"Sarah Thomas, I am arresting you on suspicion of acting as a co-conspirator in the death of Barry McGleam. You are also being charged with Concealing Evidence and making false statements to a police officer."

Hale turned toward the officer. "Officer, please take Ms. Thomas into custody and recite her Miranda rights."

Begley looked on as the officer handcuffed the weeping Sarah Thomas. He made a notation in his log, then put down his pen as the officer commenced to recite the Miranda Rights.

"Come with me, Ms. Thomas," he said. As he escorted her from the interrogation room to a holding cell.

Hale turned toward Begley. "Mr. Begley, you may begin your defense immediately. I will arrange for an arraignment hearing as soon as possible. You can contact the District Attorney's office for information on the hearing's schedule."

Begley packed his paperwork into a leather briefcase and walked out of the room. It was obvious to both Ralph and me that he had his hands full with Sarah's defense.

After Begley's departure, we waited a minute before leaving the observation room. Hale met us as we passed his desk on our way out. A smug look dominated his face. He wasn't happy that he had to charge Sarah Thomas first before he caught up with Jason Callahan. But the District Attorney's office was breathing down his neck. With Sarah's arrest, he finally had something to show for his work.

Next on his list, he wanted to catch the big fish, Jason Callahan.

I didn't fully understand Hale's process. What was taking so long? "Why haven't you brought Jason in?" I asked. "Now that you have Sarah in custody, he might make a run for it."

"Don't worry, we have him under surveillance. I am awaiting the results of some lab tests. It will probably be tomorrow before we know for sure. I'll text you Mr. Dowden when something happens."

With nothing to do but wait for Hale to make his arrest of Jason Callahan we returned to Ralph Dowden's house to await the next day's events.

JESSICA RETURNS HOME

I spent another sleepless night pondering Sarah Thomas' arrest and the pending arrest of Jason Callahan. Suddenly, everything was happening fast, progress was finally being made.

After breakfast, I returned to visit Jessica in her hospital room. Jessica's recovery was only beginning, yet she already showed signs of improvement. With the help of her nurse and the nurse's assistant, she moved from the bed to sitting in a chair. The nurse's assistant brought her a mirror and toiletries and helped her with combing her hair and brushing her teeth.

I could see the beauty I always remembered returning to her face. She appeared stronger than the day before and was talking incessantly. The Sekelskys, though exhausted, looked relieved. They welcomed me.

"Jessica, you look wonderful," I said. "How are you feeling?"

Jessica smiled weakly. "I am still full of painkillers. I don't know how I feel. At least I am thinking straight again."

She changed the subject. "The police were in to see me. It seems they are still looking for Barry's killer."

"What did you tell them?" I asked.

"Nothing. I told them I was with you. I remember nothing else from that night."

"That's good. I think the detective in charge, Lieutenant Hale, is building a case. Charges are coming, soon."

I didn't want to tell her about Sarah Thomas, Barry's death, or the police's actions. I was worried about her recovery. "What are the doctors telling you?"

A few more days here in the hospital, then two weeks in a skilled nursing facility. If I do well with my therapy, I can continue my recovery at home. I can receive home visits from nurses and physical therapists during the day. I can't wait to get out of this place."

Marian Sekelsky chimed in. "I'll stay with Jessica at her house for a month or two until she can manage on her own. George is flying home on Saturday. It's been nearly two weeks. Our longest time away from home."

"What? Why aren't you coming home, Jess?" I asked. "Home to Berwyn."

"Able, I am home. I live here. I have a house, I have friends. Barry may be gone, but Norfolk is my home. Berwyn hasn't been home for over ten years. I'm staying here. Besides, now I have a job."

Her plans made no sense. I thought she wanted to return to a life free from politicians and lawyers.

It bothered me she wanted to stay in Norfolk. More so, the last part of her statement confused me. "Job, what do you mean job?"

"This morning, Tommy Boyle came here to the hospital. The governor asked him to delay his retirement and continue as District Attorney until they can schedule an interim election. It will probably be next year.

"We talked a while about my recovery and my plans. He offered me Barry's job in the District Attorney's office. He believes with a little seasoning and low-profile campaigning; I can be the party's candidate for District Attorney to replace him.

"The only opposition is Wallace Bolton. Tommy thinks I can defeat him in the special election."

Jessica's words hit me like a tidal wave. I tried to argue. "But what about us, Jess? You came to me for help. I risked my life for you. Jessica, you need to come home to Berwyn. Jessica, I love you. I have always loved you. You know that."

"I love you too Able. You're my best friend. The one I could always count on. But I have always wanted more. You know that. I will never be happy in Berwyn, and if I'm not happy, you won't be happy."

It would have hurt less if she had taken an ice pick and stabbed me in my heart. Her rejection, once again, left me torn between anger and anguish. I didn't know how to respond. I ran from the hospital room in a state of speechlessness and confusion. I asked myself, "What was it all for?"

Stepping out into the hallway, my temples pulsed in rhythm to the beat of my heart. Then, a dizzying feeling overwhelmed me. I found a chair just before my weakening legs gave out. I plopped down in time to avoid collapsing on the hard tile floor.

Sitting alone in the hallway, I held my head in my hands. Unable to hold it together, my eyes filled with tears. Before I could comprehend what had just happened, a voice called out. "Able." I looked up to see George Sekelsky standing over me. George knew what had happened in Jessica's hospital room.

"I am sorry, young man. Jessica has always been strong-willed. She always had lofty ideals. She always wanted to be rich and famous."

George reached out to hug me.

"I want you to know you are like a son to me. You are welcome in our home anytime."

"Thank you, George." I wiped my eyes. "I have to go."

I sat behind the wheel of my rental car rehashing what seemed like a never-ending saga. I tried to rationalize everything that had happened. Thoughts of anger, hatred, revenge, and forgiveness swirled through my head. "How could I be so blind?"

Just days earlier, I promised myself that if I survived this ordeal; I would break the stranglehold Jessica had on me. Now that it happened, I wavered. I could not bear to part with her.

I remembered a prayer my mom taught me when I was a boy. It was a prayer for understanding and enlightenment. She told me, "If you are ever sad or unhappy, this prayer will help."

I recited the prayer over and over, hoping my mom's faith would settle my mind.

Despite the emotional drain, Jessica was right. We weren't compatible. We were high school sweethearts who took separate paths. I was clinging to a false hope of a future together. I decided I needed to live my life on my terms, not hers.

Nearly an hour passed before I finally mustered the courage to start the car. Putting it in gear, I hit the gas and turned the wheel north towards Natick and Ralph Dowden's house.

I drove slowly, taking back roads, avoiding traffic and people, trying to vanquish my disillusionment. Cruising the rural terrain, I noticed something I hadn't observed since landing at Logan International Airport. The birch and maple trees that dominated the landscape were turning color. In the last few days, their fall red and yellow hues surged to the forefront. Their time to change arrived, as did mine. The symbolism of their transition and mine were uncanny. The trees, though healthy and growing, would soon shed their beauty and go into hibernation. They'll revive when winter fades, bigger and more beautiful. So, like them, I must shed my past. The time had come to rework myself, yet again returning to become bigger and more bountiful.

* * *

As I turned north up Route 27, I picked up my phone and dialed a familiar number.

I hadn't spoken to Thelma Jenkins in several days. Our time-out could have several explanations. One was Thelma had everything under control. Or new clients aren't reaching out for my services. Perhaps she hasn't scheduled any new client interviews until I confirm my return to Berwyn? I had to call her for an update on matters at home.

"Thelma, it's me. How are things in Berwyn?"

"Oh, Mr. Body, I have a lot to tell you. Mr. Zermenski has officially closed the title company; he moved his filing cabinets and computers out yesterday. He is leasing out the office space. It will be home to a new insurance business."

"I guess it was just a matter of time. What kind of people are we talking about?" I asked.

"It is a new insurance agency. Owned by a young woman. I met her yesterday when she came to look the place over. She seems nice. She is going to hire her own receptionist. They will use the other desk in the outer offices. Some furnishings will need to be rearranged. She is waiting for an okay from the state licensing bureau to start. It won't open for business for a couple of weeks."

Being always suspicious, I instructed Thelma. "Check her out. Let me know what we are dealing with."

"I already did. I found her agency's new website and her social media profile. Her name is Sovana Trostel. The agency is S.T. Assurance. Looking at her website, it appears she brokers specialty insurance for fine art, collectibles, and intellectual property. She has several high-end clients. I don't expect a lot of walk-in traffic. I'll text you the link to her website and her social media profile."

My conversation with Thelma was short, only two minutes. In that two-minute window, my phone rang twice. I didn't answer either call, choosing to let them go to voicemail. One call came from Ralph. "He probably wants to know if I'll be back in time for dinner." I thought. The second call came from Marian Sekelsky. I had recently left them at the hospital. I chalked it up to Marian calling to soothe my broken heart.

Twenty minutes later, I parked in front of Ralph's house. My goal was to get online and book a flight home. My work in Massachusetts was done.

Before I went into Ralph's house, I checked the message that Marian Sekelsky left. The message was brief, but panic dominated her voice.

"Able, the police were here. They read Jessica her rights. There is a police officer stationed outside her room. They made us leave the hospital. We can't see her or talk to her. Able, help us."

The message made no sense. I was sure she was confused. Before calling Marian back, I needed to talk to Hale. I had to find out what the hell he was doing.

Before I could get out of the car, Ralph stepped out his front door. He moved quickly, about as determined as I had ever seen him, towards the driver's side of the car.

"I tried calling you. Hale arrested Jason Callahan. The police found gunshot residue on a pair of pants and a shirt they pulled from his apartment."

"I'm not surprised," I said.

"Wait, there's more. He is also charging Jessica McGleam with conspiracy to commit murder."

His words stopped me in my tracks. "What? How can that be? Jessica was with me the night of the murder."

"Yes, but apparently, before she came to see you in Berwyn, she used her feminine wiles to persuade Callahan to kill Barry. She convinced Jason she was in love with him. He thought with Barry out of the way, she would marry him."

I couldn't believe what I was hearing. Hale must be way off base.

"Jeez, did Callahan think Jessica liked him? How creepy is that?"

"I know. This Jason character is really a sicko," said Ralph.

"This can't be right. Let's call Hale. I need to talk with him," I said.

We ran into the house and to Ralph's office. I watched him dial Hale's number, and to our surprise, Hale answered.

Activating the speaker on the phone, Ralph said. "Lieutenant Hale, it's Ralph Dowden, and I have Able Body with us on the line. Can you give us an update on what is happening?"

"I figured you guys would be calling. I don't want to talk about this case on the phone. Join me at my desk in the station, and we can retreat to a quiet room."

I wanted to bark out my disapproval of his actions, but Ralph held up his hand to stop me.

Instead, I held my tongue responding with a simple, "On our way."

In seconds, we were back in the car and on our way to Dedham, again.

Upon arrival at the Norfolk County Sheriff's office, Ralph and I hurried upstairs to Lieutenant Hale's desk. I needed some straightforward answers to what Hale was doing.

Hale was nowhere to be found. One of the other detectives shuttled us to a private room. It was a room for meetings rather than interrogations, equipped with a large table, whiteboard, and soft comfortable leather chairs, not the hard metal ones like the interrogation room.

"Wait here. Lieutenant Hale is on a conference call with the District Attorney. He'll get to you as soon as he can."

Confused by the sudden turn of events, we sat wondering where Hale's investigation was going. I thought the police solved the case. I thought it was cut and dried. "What changed?"

Without Lieutenant Hale present, we could speak candidly without interference. Ralph and I rehashed the series of events, trying to determine how the latest pieces of this puzzle were coming together.

Ralph kept glancing at his watch. "What the hell can he be doing?"

"I hope he has something solid," I said.

Nearly forty minutes later, Hale appeared in the room, his hands filled with manila folders and stacks of paperwork. He was all business.

He stood there towering over us like he was conducting a seminar. "I know you guys think I have been sitting on my hands.

You were wrong. My team and I have been busy sorting this whole thing out. Unlike you, we cannot afford to get this wrong. I think we finally have all the pieces together."

Hale was still sporting that arrogance that comes with being a police Lieutenant.

"We have just taken Jason Callahan into custody for the murder of Barry McGleam and the attempted murder of Jessica McGleam. We are also charging him with the road rage incident and crash that put you and Jessica in the hospital.

"Jason had a motive. He blamed Barry for his father's death. He had the means. We believe we have sufficient evidence to prove he fired the gun that killed Barry and caused your car crash. We also know he left Wallace Bolton's campaign offices the night of Barry's shooting, and we know he followed you to the Stoney Brook Wildlife Area shortly after police found Barry's body. Jason has no alibi. He's toast."

I listened, then nodded.

Lieutenant Hale continued. "As you know, we have also charged Sarah Thomas with conspiracy and providing false evidence in Barry McGleam's murder. She aided Jason after he killed Barry and tried to frame Tiffany Burns for the murder. Her motives are simple. She wanted to help Wallace Bolton, whom she loves, and to help Jason get away with the crime by deflecting the blame on Tiffany. It's complicated, but I anticipate a plea that will result in her being imprisoned for several years.

Ralph watched as I fidgeted in my seat. We were aware of Jason Callahan and suspected the case was more complex than expected. Still, Hale was dragging his feet on explaining Jessica's charges.

He continued to dance around the question I most wanted answered.

"Although I strongly suspect that Wallace Bolton had full knowledge of everything, the District Attorney is choosing not to prosecute him. There is not enough solid evidence to demonstrate his involvement beyond the cover-up. No doubt he has a motive to see Barry dead. However, he can provide evidence of his presence at his campaign headquarters during the time of death. We have no call logs, videotape, or money trail to pin him with anything except being Sarah's sounding board. The District Attorney is reluctant to charge him with a cover-up, not wanting to disturb a fellow member of the bar. He says the publicity will hurt Bolton more than a trial we may not win."

I couldn't wait any longer. I jumped up from my chair. "What the hell is happening with Jessica? Why are you charging her? I thought we agreed she was innocent?"

"No, you believed she was innocent. I thought she was guilty from the start. I just couldn't prove it. You helped me do that."

"What do you mean?" I disputed.

Hale snapped, "Sit down and be patient. I am coming to that part."

"While you guys were busy using the old-school approach to finding evidence, one of the young CSIs in our digital forensics lab was busy building a profile of Jessica's financial dealings and her interaction with Callahan and Thomas. It turns out Jessica was giving Jason money."

He opened up a manila folder filled with pictures and scanned documents. "Our evidence shows that Jessica convinced Jason of her love for him, proposing a future together if Barry was no longer in the picture."

Hale tossed a sheet of paper onto the desk. "Look at this. On two separate occasions, she paid Callahan's rent. Except that she screwed up. The rental agency would not accept cash, so she wrote a check on Callahan's behalf."

He pulled a picture of Jessica seated at a bar with Callahan. "She took him out to expensive nightclubs. We have pictures, videos, and witnesses. She bought him drugs and booze. The bartenders at the clubs remembered the two of them hanging out, getting drunk until the bar closed."

Pointing at Hale and pounding on the table in protest, I said, "Are you saying that Jessica was having an affair with a loser like Jason Callahan? You must be out of your mind."

Shaking his head, Hale responded, "No, I'm not. I don't think it was a love affair in the physical sense. They met in public places. It's easy to manipulate Jason. He didn't realize she was just leading him on. She was getting his hopes up. She played him for a patsy."

Holding up his hands and shrugging, Hale continued. "I'll admit, in the beginning, I believed that Jessica McGleam's motive was Barry's womanizing. I thought it was Barry's affair with Tiffany Burns that drove her to kill Barry. That was only partly true. Jessica had her eye on the same District Attorney's office that Barry was running for. She sensed if Barry was out of the picture, Tommy Boyle would offer her the job. It was a power grab.

"Jessica saw her chance when she learned Barry was breaking up with Tiffany for the new girlfriend. She planned a complicated scheme to frame Tiffany Burns.

"Convincing Jason to kill Barry solved two problems."

Counting with his fingers, he said. "One, Jessica gets back at Barry for cheating on her, and two, it wrecks what's left of Bolton's chances to get elected. Afterward, she gets her law career back and becomes the power broker she always wanted to become."

Turning to me he said, "She even suckered you, Body. She made you, her alibi. The one thing she hadn't counted on was the accident and a deeper investigation."

His words angered me. I was having one of the worst days of my life and Hale busily pointed it out. My insides churned but I refused to react and reveal my emotions. I kept silent.

Hale was on a roll. He kept talking. "From the start, it bothered me that Jessica knew Barry was dead when she picked you up at the airport. I kept asking myself. "How could she know?" The call Tiffany made didn't come to the emergency number until 7:32 p.m. We put it together when we found Jessica's phone on the ground near the airport. Jason texted Jessica at 6:46 p.m. The text was only three words. "No more Barry".

"No one would suspect her. She was with you, at the airport, pretending to be running away. Except that someone – whether it was Thomas or Bolton – made Callahan realize Jessica was playing him for a sucker.

"When Jason saw the two of you drive by Bolton's campaign office, with you behind the wheel of Jessica's car, it must have triggered his rage. In his anger, he tried to kill Jessica. Body, you were just collateral damage."

Ralph mumbled, "Means, Motive, and Opportunity."

Hale nodded. "Yep, now you guys are getting it. Jessica had two motives. Revenge and greed. A deranged Jason Callahan provided her with the means. When she found out that Barry was alone with his new girlfriend at his campaign headquarters, that was her opportunity."

I hated that asshole, Barry. He had all these beautiful women, and he still wasn't satisfied. "Who is this new girlfriend?" I asked.

"Another dancer, a girl from the Senator's Club. She goes by the stage name Barbie Manfor. We questioned her and grilled her pretty well. She convinced us that Barry and she were an item. When he invited her to his campaign headquarters, she believed they were going out on a date. She thought Barry was taking her out to dinner. When she realized Barry only wanted to have sex with her in his office, she left. She is smarter than the other women Barry wooed.

"Jessica McGleam is under arrest. She will be arraigned before a judge tomorrow morning in her hospital room. Her lawyer will enter a plea of not guilty.

"Because her current physical condition has her confined to her hospital room, she is not a flight risk. Based on her record and status in the community, the judge will probably grant her bail."

Hale paused for a second, half expecting me to protest again. I didn't.

"What's next?" I asked.

"The next phase of the indictment begins. Because of her close relationship with District Attorney Tommy Boyle, they will probably move the trial out of Norfolk County."

Realizing he still maintained his imposing stance, Hale grabbed a chair and sat down at the head of the table, bringing himself to eye level with us. He proceeded to summarize his story.

"Everything I have told you is based on the facts at hand."

Placing his hand on his stack of manila folders, he said. "We have the proof right here in these files. The District Attorney's office believes we will convict Jason, Jessica, and Sarah."

I could only bow my head in resignation. I spent my whole life from the time I was a freshman in high school pursuing Jessica Belle Sekelsky-McGleam. She always wanted more than I could give her. In the end, she would trade my well-being, even willing to trade my life, in her quest for money and status.

My roller coaster ride with Jessica was coming to an end. It wasn't the way I wanted it, but it was reality.

I stiffened my back, took a deep breath, and glanced at Ralph, then back at Hale. I wondered what they were thinking of me. They probably thought, Able Body was a classic fool who let a beautiful woman manipulate him, and that I wasn't any smarter than Jason Callahan. In my defense, at least I didn't kill anyone for her. What they didn't know was that I already made peace with my stupidity during the drive from the hospital.

It was too late to worry about what other people thought of me. I said the only intelligent thing possible. "Thank you, Lieutenant Hale. As much as it hurts to hear, I want to see justice done."

Hale knew I was hurting. His demeanor changed and his human side came out. "Mr. Body, I am sorry it turned out this way. Sometimes the wheels of justice don't stay on the tracks. That is the business we have chosen."

That was the end of Hale's oratory. I turned to Ralph and said, "Ralph, I cannot thank you enough for everything you have done for me. We wouldn't have solved this case without your help."

"We make a good team," Ralph replied.

"I will have Thelma Jenkins invoice Jessica Sekelsky-McGleam for every penny we have spent. I don't know if we will get paid, considering the circumstances."

"Body, you have given me the best last chapter of my book that I could ever have imagined. That's payment enough."

Turning my attention back toward Hale, I said. "Do you think they will subpoena me to testify at these trials?"

"Yes, I do. If Callahan maintains his guilty plea, his trial should go quickly. That won't be the situation with Jessica's trial. She will mount a defense that will almost assuredly drag on for months. You'll be back here to testify several times."

Ralph said, "I'll keep your room available."

For the first time since we met, Lieutenant Hale seemed genuinely contented. No fidgeting, no arrogance. Standing up, he reached out and shook both our hands.

"Gentlemen, thank you for your hard work. You are a credit to your profession. We will be in touch."

✳ ✳ ✳

I still had one problem. I needed to respond to Marian Sekelsky's voicemail. I was stalling because I couldn't do anything to help her. It was cowardly, but as I dialed, I wished the call would go to voicemail. It didn't, she answered on the second ring.

"Able, what is happening?" I could hear her voice cracking as she said, "They have arrested Jessica."

"Mrs. Sekelsky, I'm sorry. The police have evidence. I can't help Jessica. Only her lawyers and God can help her now."

The phone went silent.

I repeated, "Marian, I'm sorry." Then I hung up.

For now, the saga has ended. Jessica sowed her own seeds. She must reap the results. The murder charge she faces is serious, and Hale appears to have enough evidence for conviction. Yet, deep down inside, I knew Jessica would somehow figure a way out of this situation. Only she will do it without Able Body.

Ralph and I left the Norfolk County police station each feeling differently about the outcome.

Ralph held his head high. Only days ago, Hale referred to him as an "old has-been gumshoe". Ralph showed himself to be competent and still relevant. His story was one of excitement and success.

My mood was far more melancholy. I tried to hide my disillusionment by staring straight ahead without making eye contact with anyone. Jessica played me for a fool, yet I found it hard to accept that I had done anything wrong.

After a few minutes of silence, I turned to Ralph. "As soon as I can get a flight, I am heading back home."

"How about one last bowl of chili before you go?" he asked.

We headed back to Ralph's. He made the chili while I scoured the travel sites for an inexpensive flight back home. I found a flight for that evening. In seven hours, I would be back in Berwyn, Illinois, where I belonged.

I told Ralph before we parted company. "Before I leave for the airport, I want to call Thelma Jenkins to let her know what's happening."

I opened my laptop and initiated a video call. Seconds later, a smiling Thelma Jenkins appeared on my screen. The warmth of her bright smile against her dark skin was one of the most welcoming sights I had seen in days.

In the background, I could see the rich wood paneling and familiar old-world charm of our Berwyn offices.

"Hello, Mr. Body Are you on your way home?"

"In a few hours Thelma. How are things in Berwyn?"

"Fine. I booked an appointment for you to interview a new client tomorrow at 4:00 p.m. She believes her husband and her sister are having an affair. It's a nice way to ease back into your old routine."

"That's fine. Any updates on the new tenant?"

Thelma nodded. "She's right here. Why don't you ask her yourself?"

Thelma swiveled her computer around to face the other direction. The laptop's built-in camera captured the image of a woman, who seemed to be in her early thirties, busily unpacking boxes. She had a stack of manila folders atop a filing cabinet that needed to be organized.

The view from my laptop screen was one of a strikingly attractive woman dressed in tight black jeans and a light blue V-neck T-shirt that accented her hourglass figure. Her dark hair was styled into a chic pixie cut, and her skin had a warm, sun-kissed hue. The image momentarily took my breath away.

She broke away from her unpacking and turned toward the camera.

"Hello, Mr. Bōdyē. I'm Sovana Trostel. Thelma has told me all about you. I cannot wait for us to meet."

When she spoke, I detected an ever so slight Eastern European accent. Sovana moved closer to the screen. She looked even prettier up close. Beads of sweat formed on my forehead.

It did not go unnoticed that she called me by my proper name. Unsure what to say. I said, "Hi Sovana, I look forward to working with you."

Sovana beamed with a flirtatious smile. "When you get settled back home, let's do lunch."

Then she jokingly said, "I can use an Able Body to help validate some of the claims my office receives. Especially the theft and fraud claims. I just moved here from upstate New York, and I don't have many friends here in Berwyn."

"I am looking forward to it," I said.

I looked at Ralph, hovering nearby, and grinned. If I played my cards right, Sovana Trostel and I might become close friends, maybe more.

Ralph smiled. "That didn't take long. It seems like you're opening another door. You're lucky, your future is ahead of you. I have a feeling things are going to work out better for you, from now on."

✳ ✳ ✳

With Jessica's drama behind me, it was time to return to Berwyn. Before I parted company with Ralph, we went to dinner at an upscale steak house, my treat. It was the least I could do. He had gone above and beyond to help me and paid for much of it out of his bank account.

Later that evening, I boarded the red-eye flight out of Boston. The last two weeks have been a series of life-changing moments. I should be looking toward the future. Yet, I remained dejected.

My life was a lie. As a boy, I was a joke. Able Body, the boy with the funny name. In high school, I overcame the jokes to become a superstar. I went on to college and laid out a path for success. The future seemed unlimited.

Then I woke up one day, and it wasn't. My chosen partner was gone and everything I planned for went with her.

I became a cliche, struggling to make ends meet and to find the happiness I sought.

My father once told me, "A man must be able to look at himself in the mirror and like what he sees." I couldn't. At least not yet.

It was time to put the cliche, Able Body, and the past uncertainty behind me. Rekindling my friendship with Ralph Dowden reminded me, "Life's a long song." Real success doesn't come overnight, and the road to happiness is filled with twists and turns.

My business had everything necessary to succeed. When I got home to Berwyn, I would redouble my efforts to be the best private investigator possible.

The success I had working with UltaESurety and Kaylee Murphy, coupled with the entry of Sovana as my office neighbor, presented opportunities to recreate my investigative agency with a business model that would be the envy of my trade. I needed to get home and start again.

HOME AGAIN

I arrived back in Berwyn at 5:00 a.m. Instead of going to my apartment, I went straight to my office to see what I had missed while I was gone. Thelma Jenkins was probably still home asleep. The outer office looked quite different from when I first moved in.

The landlord, Mr. Zermenski, constructed a wood and glass divider between the two sections. It offered greater privacy for clients of both companies. From the top of the stairs, a left turn takes you to my office. Turn right to enter Sovana Trostel's office. Sovana had replaced the old furniture from Zermenski's mortgage business with new modern desks and chairs. It added an image of professionalism to her business. I promised myself Thelma and I would remodel our side to match the new look.

Inside my private office, I glanced at the whiteboard where my notes from the early investigation of Jessica Belle Sekelsky's latest drama still remained in plain view. Later today, after getting some sleep, I will clean it off and stash the paperwork in a banker's box, and hopefully, never open it again.

This morning, I had only one job. I rustled through my desk drawer and found a single-edge razor blade I used for opening packages and envelopes.

On the door to my office, the words *Able Body–Your Undercover Brother* reminded me how far off track my life had become. It was time to take my career and my life seriously.

Using the razor blade, I started scraping off the letters. Minutes later, only the words "Ābel Bōdyē - Investigations" were visible. When I meet Thelma later today, I will ask her to order fresh signs for the train station and new graphics for the door.

It was a new day. Time to say goodbye to Able Body. I glanced around at my future, smiled, then locked the door and went home.

My name is Ābel Bōdyē.

ACKNOWLEDGEMENTS

The author would like to acknowledge the assistance of the
following people in making this book a reality. Without their help,
it would still be a dream.

Cover Art by TinasBookPromos

Beta Reading by Sherilyn Lipke

Beta Reading by Rachelle Fried

Finally, I would be remiss if I didn't acknowledge my lovely wife,
Sherry. She puts up with my countless hours of typing and deleting
words on a keyboard while important chores go unfinished.
Thanks, Sherry.

What do a Civil Engineer, a small-town Police Chief, and a rich widow all have in common?

They all want to expose political corruption, solve a murder, and bring the bad guys to justice.

Engineer Joseph DiMarco has unearthed a scheme to steal millions of dollars in taxpayer money. When DiMarco goes missing, his former business partner, Ned Tabor, begins an investigation.

Tabor enlists the help of a small-town Police Chief and a band of enterprising private citizens to help him unravel the mystery. With only brains and cunning Ned and his friends work to solve the puzzle. The result is a chain of events that will have you guessing how it will all end.

The DiMarco Incident is an intriguing story filled with "ah-ha" moments. You won't put it down.

And

Saint Joseph

Investigative Journalist, D.K. St. Joseph believes the best place to hide a tree is in the forest.

He sets the journalism community on fire with his outside-the-box reporting and revealing exposés. Traveling the globe from the streets of the inner city to the jungles of India, he is determined to find the hidden truth in every story.

When he takes on a corrupt politician and forces his resignation, the world takes notice. His investigations into corporate greed and money laundering nominated him for awards.

Asked to put a new spin on a widely reported homicide investigation, life changes for St. Joseph. His efforts to help free an innocent man introduce him to a beautiful woman with a hidden past. The affair shatters his innocence and makes him question his sanity.

Follow St. Joseph as he learns that success and happiness come from people and relationships, not fame and fortune.

About The Author

J. Salvatore Domino is an award-winning author and blogger based in Scottsdale, Arizona, U.S.A.

His journey from technical writing to the boundless realm of fiction is a testament to the power of transformation.

Demonstrating his storytelling prowess, he captivates the reader, inviting them into a world where the lines between the imagined and the real are artfully blurred. His tales span a spectrum from comforting to thrilling, while his characters are crafted to evoke strong reactions, mirroring the complexities of real-life individuals.

His notable works include the cyber-crime series "The Algorithm Man," a classic whodunit "The DiMarco Incident," and a blended mystery/romance "Saint Joseph." Collectively, they reflect his versatility and ability to connect with a diverse audience.